Catalina,
Trust God with your whole being.
Body, soul and Spirit.
He will never let you down.
You have been a joy and
I look forward to
having a great friendship!
All my love,
Jessie Xavier

I Blew God a Kiss

a novel
by

Jessie Xavier

ProphetessPublishing
CHICAGO, ILLINOIS

Published by
Prophetess Publishing
a division of
LHP Productions
P.O. Box 4062, Oak Park Illinois, 60303
Visit our website at www.lhpproductions.com

ISBN: 978-0-9789670-1-7

I Blew God a Kiss is a collaboration of a dream and the author's belief of a unified culture, regardless of race or nationality. When God created man he made him in his image. The author's aspiration is that the fighting and hostility often seen amongst man will one day come to an end. It will be sparked by a new wave of relationships—the family.

I Blew God a Kiss is a mixture of unique characters who gracefully added to the author's path of wisdom.

Other works by Jessie Xavier
"A Merry Heart Doeth Good Like a Medicine"— *A collection of jokes and inspirational stories.*

"Enter Pat's Kitchen" — *Patricia Juanita Green's collection of over 300 recipes collected over a of 30-year span.*

This is the first of many novels. A series of children's books by the author are soon to follow. It is our belief that reading any of her emotionally filled and wisdom-driven stories will touch and change your life.

This book is dedicated to the only race that God created The Human Race.

I Blew God a Kiss

I Blew God a Kiss

She held an *Alabama Chronicle* in her hands, as she stood on top of the red dirt mound. The headline read, "Local Girl Makes the Big Time." Layla Renée Porter, "hum, is that really me, a famous fashion designer." Layla thought. She could barely contain her emotions. With all the tragic events that had happened, how could this be? Was this a misprint?

Layla drifted above the cloud until she had positioned herself on her favorite nimbus. She breathed in deeply and felt the cool wind that entered her nostrils. It was *refreshing*. The heat from the sun baked her skin. Still she did not move. A little tickle up her leg caused her to twinge. Still she would not move. It was a red ant and it took a vicious bite out of her leg. She rose and hit it causing a bloodstain on her hand.

Layla's favorite pastime was to lie on top of the red dirt hill. She could stay there for hours daydreaming about becoming a fashion designer. Her sense of using the finest quality of fabrics pleased her. "Only the best," she would say to her assistant with a smile. She always knew the colors she wanted for each outfit. The models would rush around to see what she wanted them to wear. She could hear a bee buzzing around her head. First an ant now a bee, she thought, how could they get so far up in my cloud? This awoke her from her fantasy.

She opened her eyes and the forest folded itself around her like a protective shield. She trembled with fright not knowing why. She had never been afraid of being in the woods. She must have been there for hours, because the sun was going down. Her mother didn't like her going in the woods alone. As she walked back down the path she had strewn out, she tried to think of what she would say when she faced her mother. In her hand she held onto a paper bag full of red dirt. I am not giving up my dirt, she thought. "I don't know how I am going to explain this," she heard herself say. "Maybe I should throw it away and mother wouldn't know." She enjoyed the rich taste of red dirt baked fresh from the oven. So she squeezed the bag a little tighter. She crossed over a long log that had fallen over a ravine, and she knew she was almost home. She had on a lime green top and a pair of multicolor culottes. The closer she got to the house the faster she walked. She almost tripped trying to walk, while brushing the dirt and leaves from her clothes. Her hands became sweaty, and she felt a little faint. She put the bag of dirt under a broken down chair on the back porch.

As soon as she opened the door she heard her mother's goaded voice. She was holding a *True Confession* magazine in her hand.

"Ma-Me what have you done to my book?" Her mother opened it and pointed to the holes that should have shown pictures of people.

"I needed some clothes for my paper dolls they—" Layla's

I Blew God a Kiss

voice trembled.

"I am getting rid of those dad blame dolls. You need to snap out of that fantasy world you living in," she stormed away still swearing about the book that she hadn't read.

Layla looked up toward heaven and whispered, "Thank you God," her mom didn't say a word about her being late after school.

Layla's beauty was enchanting. Her skin tone was a brazen bronze like that of a person who spent weeks in a tanning salon just to get the right complexion. It was hard to distinguish her race. She had hazel eyes and long brown curly hair. She had a small mark on her right cheek the shape of a half-moon. She hated it. Her brother Jordan called it her beauty mark. Layla wondered why her complexion wasn't as dark as her family's. Her dad was a little fair skinned but nothing close to her color. Yet no one had ever made any comments about the obvious family difference. For as long as she could remember they called her Ma-Me.

It was 1967 a hard time for blacks living in Alabama and equally hard for someone like Layla. How do you rise above racial tension that's thicker than fog on a mountaintop? She spent most of her young life with her head in the clouds. Being alone was what she preferred, but her older brother Jordan was her favorite person. She couldn't image him ever not being there. He was seventeen, six years older than she was. She had two younger siblings, Juanita seven and David, who was five-years-old.

A black car dropped Jordan off. The light that glimmered from the back porch was his guide through the darkness. As he approached the porch, he spotted the brown bag under a chair. When he opened it and saw what was inside, he smiled. He put the bag under his arm and went inside and turned off the back porch light. He entered the room where his mom was asleep on the sofa. The smell of Vodka hung in the air. He covered her with a blanket and turned off the radio. The clock on the wall rang the midnight chime. His father was not home from work yet. Jordan thought, he probably won't be in until morning. As he continued down the hall, he noticed his younger brother and sister curled up next to each other fast asleep in their room. He opened the door to Layla's room and noticed a light shining under her blanket.

"Ma-Me, what are you doing up?"

"Jay Pee! I was waiting for you," she said excitedly.

"Ma-Me, what is this?" He showed her the bag.

"I wanted some red dirt."

"How many times do I have to tell you not to go in the woods alone?"

"Nothing happened! I am not scared."

"That's not the point. It's dangerous. Promise you won't go unless I am with you."

"Ohm."

"Promise Ma-Me."

"You ain't never round," she said pouting.

"I know I've been busy lately with work and school. School'll be out soon and I'll have more time."

"Okay, I'll wait for you," she gave him a hug, "will you tell me a story?"

He knelt down beside her bed. He looked up at the ceiling as if a book was there waiting to be read.

"I got it," he exclaimed, "there were two men picking blackberries."

I Blew God a Kiss

"Picking blackberries?"

"Ma-Me, I am telling this story."

"Sorry," she said apologetic.

"These two men picking blackberries—"

"How old are they?" She said yawning.

"Ma-Me you interrupt again and I am going to bed."

"Lay side me?"

Jordan climbed into bed with her and put his arms around her.

"Alright the men in the berry patch," he pulled the hair out of her face and noticed that she was asleep. He smiled and gave her a kiss on her forehead.

"Well I guess I will have to tell my berry pickin' story some other time," he said as he got out of the bed.

The next morning when Jordan got up, he knew that he would have to cook breakfast. This was his normal routine on the mornings when his mom would drink the night before. Jordan's parents were married for eighteen years. His father Joseph has worked in the cotton mills for over twenty years. His mom Sadie hadn't worked since Layla arrived.

Joseph came in while Jordan was preparing breakfast. Jordan's anger with his father had festered for many years. He blamed him for his mom's unhappiness. He tried to be polite.

"Good morning Pop," were the words he managed to utter.

"Jay Pee, has your mom been drinking again." Jordan didn't respond. He thought if you were home, she wouldn't drink. His father tried again to resume the conversation.

"Have you decided on a college yet, son?"

"No sir, I have narrowed it down to three schools," he said a little more enthusiastic.

"You still have your heart set on practicing law," his father continued.

"There is nothing else I would rather do with my life," Jordan remarked with much resistance. He felt his father's tone was condescending.

"Son a black man doesn't have a chance with this so called justice system."

"The law is fair. It is neither black nor white," Jordan shot back.

"Jay Pee, where do you get such nonsense? This is a white man's world we live in. You can't believe that."

"Yes, I believe it. Somebody has to fight to make this a better world. Why shouldn't it be me?"

His father put his head in his hands. Jordan looked up and Layla was standing in the door.

"Good morning Ma-Me," he said. He was thankful she walked in.

Joseph turned around and lifted Layla in the air. He gave her a kiss on the lips.

"How is my best girl," he said.

"Papa, where you been? I miss you," Layla said as she held on to his neck.

"Ma-Me get Nita and Davie up and wash up for breakfast," Jordan interrupted.

"I want pancakes," she said as she left the room.

Joseph turned and looked at Jordan, then walked out of the

room. Jordan bit his lip and threw the dishtowel he was holding on the table. He fought back the tears and took out the box of Aunt Jemima from the cupboard.

Saturday was Jordan's long day at work. He worked at the A&P grocery store. He stocked shelves, bagged grocery and did any other odd job that his boss could find. There had been tension between him and his boss because he didn't think that black folk should get an education. Jordan told him he would be quitting in a couple of weeks. He made plans to go to summer school to take some college prep courses. His boss, Mr. Scotty, did not take the news well. He wanted to fire him, but he was a good worker. The employees liked him and so did the customers. When Jordan walked in the store, Mr. Scotty was standing there waiting for him.

"Jordan—follow me," was all he said.

Mr. Scotty was a big man. His legs were smaller than the rest of his body. Jordan wondered how he supported his body with those legs. His clothes were not fashionable. It reminded Jordan of a teepee he saw in one of his books. Even the colors he wore were drab and dingy looking. Mr. Scotty led Jordan into the freezer.

"Jordan we just got a shipment of ham in, and I need you to make some room on these two shelves," he said as he pointed to the bottom shelves that were totally packed.

"Yes sir," Jordan replied as he thought, it is going to be a long day.

"The freezer is not a bad place to work on a hot day like today," Jordan thought.

He was trying to have a good attitude so the day would pass quickly. Jordan stepped out of the freezer after about two hours of rearranging, "stuff and mo stuff," he said as he cuffed his hand together to blow warm air into them. He looked up and he saw Layla running down the cereal isle.

"Jay Pee," she said gasping for air.

"Ma-Me, what is the matter? What happen?"

"Mama. Come… home now."

2

S adie Mae Bailey was fifteen years old when she walked into Jake's juke joint for the first time. She'd heard her sibling talk about this place since she was eleven. She was the fourth oldest child in a family of eight. She had five brothers and two sisters. That night she was with her oldest sister Juanita. They lived in a small mill town and on Friday nights the place was crowded. The mill workers who were getting off came to wind down and others were on their way to work. Sadie was nervous but watching Juanita laughing and flirting with the men helped her to relax.

There were a few round tables with chairs in the middle of the floor. On the left side of the room were a couple of booths. There was a couple in one of them sitting close. In front of her was a counter. A woman was serving drinks and preparing fish dinners for those who ordered them. To the right of her was a smaller room. In this room was a pool table, a small dance floor and the jukebox. She looked around the room to see were Juanita was. She spotted her at the counter and then headed for the jukebox.

As she searched for Billie Holiday, it was as if everything around her had disappeared. She found a dime in the side of the

I Blew God a Kiss

little gray handbag that belonged to her mother. She stood there with her eyes closed singing with the record. He walked up behind her and whispered.

"You have a nice voice."

She clinched her chest and took a deep sigh.

"Did I frighten you?" He asked.

She stood there with her mouth opened. He was knock down gorgeous. His hair was jet-black and wavy. He had combed it back, so you could see those beautiful eyes, she thought. When he smiled, it was as if his teeth sparkled.

Then he said it again, "Did I frighten you?"

"No... I mean yea... I was—"

"I interrupted your song. I'll play it for you again."

Oh my goodness, she thought. If my heart doesn't stop beating so fast, I am going to die!

"My name is Joseph Porter. I have never seen you in here before."

"My sista Juanita—" she said nudging her head in Juanita's direction.

"Yeah, I know Nita." He leaned over and whispered in her ear, "You are much prettier.

"What's your name suga?"

"Sadie."

"Sadie Mae."

"No, just Sadie, don't like Sadie Mae."

"Okay pretty lady I won't call you Sadie Mae."

He played another selection.

"Let's dance honey," he held out his hand. He was forceful

yet smooth and without hesitation she reached for his hand. He pulled her close to him.

"You don't need to tremble. I won't hurt you." On their way home Sadie could think of nothing but Joseph and his smile. Juanita was talking nonstop, but she didn't hear a word Juanita said.

"You hear me," Juanita yelled.

"What'd you say?"

"You stay away from that Joe Porter—he ain't no good."

"What?" Sadie giggled.

"Stay away from him. You hear!"

When they walked into the house, Lizzie met them at the door.

"What is all that noise?" Lizzie asked.

"Your sista been bit by the Joe Porter bug," Juanita said as she threw her hands in the air.

Lizzie was seventeen and didn't go out much but she had heard stories about how Joe treated women.

"Lord Chile," she said, "you need ta listen ta Nita. You"ll only get hurt."

"That's silly, goodnight," Sadie said with a smile.

When Sadie got into bed, she thought, they are just jealous. He thinks I am prettier than they are; besides, he said he wouldn't hurt me.

As Sadie nursed her bruises, she thought about that night twenty years ago when she first met Joseph Porter.

"Why did I not listen to my sisters," she said as she licked the blood from her lips.

She looked up and Jordan was standing at the bathroom door.

I Blew God a Kiss

"You alright," he said as he started to reach for her.

She put her hand up to stop him from coming toward her.

"What you doing home?"

"Ma-Me came to the store—"

"For what? I am going to kick her butt."

"Oh this Ma-Me's fault?"

"Jay Pee you ain't my daddy," she said rolling her eyes sharply at him.

Jordan shook his head and walked back into the living room. The place was a mess. Broken plates and glass was all over the floor. The tables and chairs were knocked over. Layla stood in the middle of the floor with one arm around David and the other around Juanita.

Jordan smiled at the children and said, "hey let's go sit on the porch."

The front porch had an old rusted iron swing. It was an olive green but the paint had begun to peel. Rust and what was once red paint showed through in spots.

Jordan picked up Juanita and put her on his lap. Layla sat down and put her head on his shoulder. David sat on the opposite side of him.

"Way we goin taday, Jay Pee," David said as he looked with wide eyes at his brother.

"Where you want to go Nita?" Jordan asked his baby sister.

"I want ta go ta Naw'leans," she smiled excitedly.

"New Orleans, home of the Madi Gras."

The porch swing was a place that with a good imagination they could travel all over the world and back in less than an hour.

Jordan began to rock back and forwards as he traveled in his mind to New Orleans. He began to talk about the Dixieland band and the cruise on the Mississippi River. He toured the Vieux Carre' and took a buggy ride around the French Quarter admiring the huge plantation homes. He talked of the exciting night, the lights, and the laughter of the people as they prepared for the Madi Gras. He pointed to the costumes and asked, "Have you ever seen anything more beautiful?" He described the colors and the fabrics and the incredible masks. Then he was exhausted and hungry for a muffuletta.

"Let's go again," Nita said.

"Yeah, let's go ta The Yok," David said.

"No I don't like New York," Layla said.

"Okay, that's enough, Ma-Me take them inside," Jordan stood up and motioned them toward the door.

"Where you going?" Layla knew that Jordan's mind was not on the trip to New Orleans. She knew that he wanted to find their father.

"I'll be back," he said.

"Want me to call Nanmu?" Layla asked.

"Ma-Me, don't worry."

"Where you going?"

Jordan turned around and walked back up the stairs. He put his hand on Layla's cheek and said, "I told you don't worry."

Layla took her brother and sister back into the house. She looked around at the mess and thought. I'll fix them a sandwich and give them a glass of milk. Then I'll clean this mess up.

She looked up and her mom was coming down the hall. She had put on some make-up that hid the bruises well.

I Blew God a Kiss

"Ma-Me, clean this mess up."

"Yes, mam."

"I am going out for a spell."

"Mama you alright?"

She leaned down and pinched Layla's arm fiercely.

"Look Ma-Me, you didn't have to go get Jay Pee. I can handle Joseph."

Layla nodded biting her lower lip.

"I'll be back in a couple of hours," she said as she opened the front door.

David hit Juanita and ran through the living room. Juanita yelled and chased him around the room.

"Stop that!" Layla screamed, "go in the kitchen so I can fix you somein eat!" Layla yelled with tears in her eyes.

"Ma-Me why you cryin?" Nita asked.

"I'm not cryin. Get in the kitchen," she said as she wiped her tears.

Layla finished the sandwiches and then started cleaning the living room. She knew that her mom was right, she could handle her father. Sadie often started the fights out of her frustration of wanting Joseph to change his ways. The fights occurred when Joseph had been away from home for days. Sadie would demand to know where he had been and with whom. His response was mostly the same, "Gawn woman and leave me alone," he would say. Then she would get angry and pick up a shoe, or whatever was close, and throw it at him. Sometimes he would just laugh but sometimes, like today, he would get mad. He would always repeat the same words when he hit her, "Don't I take care of you and these here chilin? What do you what from me?" Then he would leave again.

Grassy Creek was a small town, so Layla knew where he would go. At the moment the most recent woman was Melanie Foster. She did hair out of her home but rumor was that since Joe Porter started hanging around her she didn't do much hair anymore. Layla remembered when she and Jordan saw Melanie in the A&P.

"Y'all Joe Porter's youngan's?" She asked, knowing who they were.

"Yesem," Jordan replied.

"Y'all some fine, chillin."

"Thank you Mam."

She was cordial and Jordan was civil with her. He didn't like her at all. She was a few years older than him. Her clothes were half a size too small, exposing firm breast and a tightly round bottom. Jordan always thought she was too lovely to walk around looking as if she was selling herself. She reminded him of the ladies who walked down on Bakker Street. He often wondered if that's where his father had found her.

Layla had just finished picking up the last piece of glass and organizing the last piece of furniture when her mom came in. She had been drinking, and had a brown bag in her hand.

"Ma-Me can you fix me some eggs," she said as she walked down the hall toward the bedroom.

Juanita ran out of the kitchen. David followed her laughing and throwing his shoe at her. Layla ignored them and headed toward the kitchen.

Jordan came in through the back door and was roaming through the refrigerator when Layla entered the kitchen.

"Jay Pee, how long you been here?" Layla asked surprised to see him.

I Blew God a Kiss

Jordan sighed sounding tired, "I just walked in," he said.

"I need to fix Mama some eggs."

"She been drinking?"

Layla took a deep breath and said, "yeah."

"Look after your brother and sister. I'll fix her something."

"Jay Pee did you see Papa?"

"No."

"Did you go back to work?"

"No."

"Where you been?"

Layla's questions was annoying Jordan. When he looked in her face he smiled.

"Ma-Me, I have always wondered why we call you Ma-Me. Now I know."

She threw her arms around him and said, "I love you, Jay Pee."

"I love you too Ma Me."

Layla left the kitchen only to return minutes later.

"Jay Pee there's some policemen at the door," she said.

"Police. What do they want?"

"They're asking for you."

Jordan followed Layla into the living room. There stood two officers. One was big and rough looking. He held a stick in his hands. The other officer was young and handsome. He was tall and slim with smooth skin, and he did the talking.

"My name is Officer Ryan. Are you Jordan Porter?"

"Yes sir, I am."

"We would like for you to come down to the station to answer some questions."

"What is this about, sir?"

"Someone robbed the A&P and we need you to answer some questions."

"I left work—"

"Son, there won't be any trouble if you just come with us."

"Am I under arrest?" Jordan asked.

The other officer spoke up, "Are you coming nicely or do I have to put these cuffs on you?"

Jordan turned to Layla and said, "Ma-Me get Mama."

Layla returned with their mom and the big rugged looking policeman was putting handcuffs on Jordan.

"Sam, get those cuffs off him! There is no need for that," Officer Ryan was saying.

Sadie came in demanding to know what they wanted with her boy.

Officer Ryan spoke, "Mam, we just want to ask him a few questions."

"Well ask him," she said as she put her hands on her hips.

"Mam we need him to come to the station."

"I have a good boy. What's he pose to done?"

Jordan interjected, "Mama, I haven't done anything. I swear."

Officer Ryan was getting impatience, "Mrs. Porter," he said, "if he comes to the station with us—we'll answer all your questions.

"Alright if I come?" Sadie asked.

"Yes Mam that would be fine."

Sadie told Ma-Me to call Nanmu and ask her to sit with them until they got back.

Juanita Watson and David Bailey met while teaching in Tuskegee. At the time they were activist for the plight of the Negro. They fought along side W.E.B. Du Bois, Dr. Martin Luther King, Jr. and Booker T. Washington in the NAACP for jobs, education and freedom for the Negro.

Juanita (Nanmu) stopped teaching when she started having children. She bore eight before her wellspring of life delivered her no more. The southern church was a powerful force for political activists like the Bailey family. They relied on David's status as a deacon and a speaker to inform the Negro of the significance of education. David died when their youngest son Nathaniel was two years old. She never remarried. "The Lord is my husband," she would say, "and he will provide."

She returned to teaching and tutoring, relying on the older children to take care of the younger ones. Her children from oldest to youngest are Juanita Bell, Elizabeth called, Lizzie, Martin, Sadie Mae, David Booker, Samuel Eugene, Joshua and Nathaniel Watson.

Nanmu upheld a strict regiment that allowed all her children to receive a high school diploma. Whenever they would slack in their work, she would recount how she traveled fifty miles with her daddy to help Booker T. Washington build the first coloured school in Tuskegee. "Ignorant people are takers in this world. I won't allow any of my children to be takers. You have to earn your own way," this saying was Nanmu's constant sermon to all of them.

When they were older they realized that Nanmu had embellished her story a bit. They lived only fifteen miles from Tuskegee. Fifty miles sounded a lot more heroic to travel then fifteen miles.

When Nanmu arrived, Layla had fed her brother and sister and was getting them ready for their bath. Nanmu stood there admiring Layla before she spoke.

"My, my, how you have grown," she said flashing the perfect smile.

Nanmu was a large woman about 5 feet 11 and close to three hundred pounds. She was well groomed for all occasions. She wore her hair pressed straight and pulled back in a single bun. Only on Sundays would she allow her hair to drape softly over her shoulders.

They yelled, "Nanmu," in unison and turned to give her a hug.

They hadn't seen her in a while and they all missed her. Nanmu and Sadie had a disagreement about Sadie's drinking and Joseph's carousing. Sadie cut Nanmu's heart with harsh words. "Stay out of my life and out of my business," she once told her. Nanmu asked the Lord to forgive her daughter for falling so far away from Him.

Nanmu held on to the kids for a long time and said, "Oh how

I have missed you."

"We missed you too Nanmu," they said.

"Ma-Me I'll give Davie and Nita their bath," she said.

She handed Layla a fashion magazine she had in her purse. Layla thanked Nanmu and hugged her again. Then she went to her room to cut out some paper dolls.

After Nanmu had finished giving their baths, she read them a story in the bible about David and Goliath. David loved that story because Nanmu would tell him that he was strong like David. She told him that David was just a boy when he slew the giant.

"He had great faith in what his God could do," she said.

"I got faith Nanma," David said.

"Me too!" Juanita piped in.

Nanmu laughed, "Good, now let's say our prayers and get some sleep."

She stayed in their room awhile until they fell asleep. Every once in a while she would put her hands on David's heart just to feel his heart beat. He reminded her so much of her husband whom she ached for, even after all these years.

Nanmu stood at the door of Layla's room. She listened as Layla talked to her imaginary characters. She opened the door and peaked in.

"Ma-Me, I do declare," she said, "I thought someone was in this room with you."

Layla smiled and started putting her paper dolls away. Layla's dolls were private to her. When she was alone with her dolls, it was as if she was in a perfect world where nothing or no one could do her any harm. The dolls were much company to her. Her mother didn't understand that she needed them to escape the world that had already become cruel to her. Sadie thought she was helping her daughter when she threw her dolls away. Layla didn't mind Nanmu's comment. She felt that she was the only one that understood her. Nanmu sat on the bed beside Layla and started helping her put the dolls in the shoebox where she hid them.

"It was nice of Jay Pee to give you his room," Nanmu said.

"He helped me fix it up," Layla said with a jukebox grin as she pointed to the purple drapes.

"How is he doing in the attic?"

"I don't know. He don't complain none."

"He doesn't complain much," Nanmu corrected her. "No—Jay Pee wouldn't," she said standing up with the shoebox in her hand. She put it on the dresser and picked up the comb and brush.

"My, your hair has grown. You need to keep it braided so it won't tangle so."

Layla loved it when Nanmu did her hair. The connection between them was strongest during this time. Nanmu was easy to talk to and she knew the right words to say.

"Nanmu," Layla said.

"Hmm hmm."

"Am I white?"

"Child, why do you ask such questions?"

"At school, they say I'm white. They want to know where my real parents are."

Nanmu knew that it would come a time when Layla would question her identity. Nanmu's need to tell Layla was deep and overpowering at times but she resolved to leave that task to her parents. She started talking about other things hoping that Layla would soon fall asleep.

"My hands are not as strong as they used to be," she said, "That old "Auther" is taking over. Remember how I used to get you to rub my arms and legs down for me, Ma-Me?" There was no response. Layla had fallen asleep.

When Sadie came in from the police station Joseph was with her. Nanmu had fallen asleep on the sofa. Joseph asked Sadie if he should wake her and take her home. Sadie replied that he should let her sleep until morning. Joseph went in to check on the kids. Sadie lit a cigarette and stepped out on the porch. A few minutes later Joseph joined her.

The night air was refreshingly cool. There were rows of pecan trees on the left side of the house. The right side of the house yielded a huge oak and a couple of dogwoods. The night crept along in silence except for the piercing cricket sounds.

Joseph walked up behind Sadie and put his arms around her.

"Do you remember that Billie Holiday song that was playing the night we met?" He kissed her on the cheek and then started to sing, *"I' m gonna love you like nobody's loved you come rain or come shine. High as a mountain deep as a river come rain or come shine. Happy together unhappy together and want it be fine."*

Sadie turned around. Her eyes filled with tears. She started beating Joseph on the chest.

"They got my boy!" She screamed.

Joseph cupped her hands, "Sadie honey, listen to me," he said, "haven't I always taken care of my family?" He kissed her hands.

I Blew God a Kiss

There was no response from Sadie.

"Well, haven't I," he said.

"They got my boy," she said through clenched teeth.

"You listen to me woman and listen good. You know that boy is innocent. He'll be home before you know it. As soon as the magistrate gets in on Monday, I'll get him out."

"How could Mr. Scotty say those things bout him?" Sadie asked with fire-lit eyes.

"You know that some white folk don't like to see ambitious black folk. It scares 'em."

"Why, I don't understand?"

"I don't either, woman. I think that maybe they think it will take something from their children. I don't know. What I do know is you need to get some rest. You know Nanmu has alerted the family by now and the house will be full of folk tomorrow."

"I can't sleep. I need a drink."

"Sadie, I need you sober."

"I didn't say nothing about getting drunk. I said I need a drink," she said as she pushed him away.

"Look, we not gone fight. I'll get you something," he placed his hand on her shoulder and asked her to go inside.

Joseph had a fifth of scotch in the trunk of his car. Sadie drinks vodka, he thought, but this will have to do. He closed the trunk and tucked the bottle under his arm.

No one in the Porter's house slept much that night. That was the first time that Jordan had been away all-night. Sadie was protective of him and didn't allow him to stay away from home not even overnight with Nanmu. Sadie and Layla cried most of the night.

Nanmu slept awhile and prayed awhile. She couldn't understand why a child as sweet as Jordan should have to endure such persecution.

The next day the family came in full support. The women gathered in the kitchen and the men flocked on the back porch. Nanmu and Sadie were sitting at the table. Lizzie, Juanita and Nathan's wife, Annie Mae, started removing the cover from the dishes of food they brought in. They could hear the men laughing and telling jokes through an open window. Lizzie's husband Roy was the most rowdy and every once in a while you could hear Juanita's friend Frankie saying, "Nah, nah, man that ain't right."

"I ain't lying," Roy continued, "That Pearl Jenkins was an itty-bitty ole' thang and hur sista Millie musta' wore near three hundra pound. Them's ole' pappy want let Pearl go out lesten you took Millie too. One day I took them gals down to Belle's greasy spoon for lunch. Millie order a bolono' and chees' sammich with lots of maynaze. You should've seen the look Pearl gave hur. When that gals sammich came back she opened it up and slowly scooped the maynaze off the bread wit a spoon. She sat thar licking that spoon of maynaze like it was cholate. Then she put the rest of that sammich aside."

"You lying man, you mean she didn't eat the rest of that sandwich?" Frankie asked.

"You kidding me, man as soon as she thought we want looking she stuff that sammich in hur pocket. She didn't get three hundra pound for eatin maynaze." They all laughed hysterically, except Sam Bailey.

The women were quiet. Finally Nanmu spoke to Sadie.

"When will you tell that child who she is?"

I Blew God a Kiss

"What you talking bout Nanmu," Sadie said in a dry tone.

"You know full well, what I'm talking bout. Ma-Me, when you going to tell her?"

"There is nothing to tell."

"Ma-Me is beginning to wonder. She is being teased at school."

"There is nothing to tell, Ma-Me is my chile that's all she needs to know."

"Sadie Mae, you need to tell that child the truth."

"Lay off Nanmu!" She stood up, hit her fist on the table, shoved the chair under it and stormed out of the room.

Nanmu grabbed her chest and moaned.

Juanita sat beside Nanmu and held her hand.

"She didn't mean that Nanmu, you know her and that boy is joined at the hip. That is all she is able to handle right now," Juanita said.

"I don't know where I went wrong with that child."

Lizzie piped in, "Nanmu, there is nothing you have done. Nita is right. She is just worried about the boy."

Joseph walked in the back door, "What's going on?"

"We're just worried about the boy," Annie Mae said.

Joseph kissed her on the forehead. "Well we got some hungry men back there and thirsty too."

"I'll get Ma-Me and we'll bring some tea and lemonade out," Lizzie said as she walked out of the kitchen.

Joseph joined the others on the back porch. Roy was speaking.

"I thank that's fine, let's see what Joe thank bout that."

"Let's see what Joe thinks about what?" Joseph said.

Roy continued, "Well, Sam's just saying, heck, you tell 'em Sam."

Sam stood up and told Joseph to sit down. He tried to speak with a positive attitude, but worry and concern was heard in his voice.

"Joe, I think we need to have a lawyer there when the magistrate comes in tomorrow," Sam said.

"That's nonsense," Joe said as he stood up, "why would Jay Pee need a lawyer? He is innocent. That boy never did anything wrong in his life."

"Joe listen, please sit down," Sam tried to be calm.

"I don't need to sit down. Don't you think if I thought he needed a lawyer I would have one by now."

"Joe listen to Sam, we want what's best for Jay Pee," Nathan said.

Joseph nodded and sat back down.

"Joe, you said yourself the police weren't cooperative. We don't know what charges they will try to pin on him. A woman has been shot and the A&P robbed. They will need to stick this on somebody. I want us to prepare for the unexpected. They say it was three guys. We know that Jay Pee don't hang out with a bunch of guys. I know that lawyers are not cheap. I have $200.00. Does anyone know a good lawyer we can have speak for him when we go to court?" Sam asked.

"What about that Jeff Coggins guy?" Nathan asked.

"No way man, that guy's a real jerk," Roy replied.

"I know someone that helped me out of a jam a while back,"

I Blew God a Kiss

Frankie said.

"Yeah—well who is he?" Joseph asked.

"His name is Billy Cane. He'll work with you on paying him and he got me off."

"What you do man?" Sam asked.

"I didn't do nothing man. I was innocent."

Everybody laughed.

Lizzie and Layla came out with the drinks. Layla handed Roy a glass of lemonade.

He commented on how beautiful she was.

"You gone be a molda one day gal," he said.

"No a fashion designer," she chimed back.

"And a darn good one too," Joseph said.

"I'll drink to that," Sam said holding up the glass of tea that Lizzie handed him.

I Blew God a Kiss

Monday morning finally arrived. Billy Cane met with Jordan at the courthouse. He was a rugged looking guy. He had a huge mustache that covered his top lip. There wasn't any hair on the top of his head but the back was full of curly locks that ran down his neck. He wore a suit that looked as though he'd worn it for days. Jordan was nervous when he saw him. He decided not to judge by appearance, but to give him a chance.

"Okay, let's see what we got here," Billy said as he looked over the papers in his hand, "It says here that you and two other guys walked into the A&P with loaded guns. Shot a girl while she was running out the door and escaped with... does that say one hundred fifty dollars?" He said looking for Jordan to give him an answer. Jordan didn't answer.

"Listen, I am your lawyer. I am here to help you. It doesn't matter whether you did it or not. I am going to work out the best deal for you," he said.

"I don't need no deal. I didn't do this!" Jordan exclaimed.

"Listen, son. It says here that if you hand over those other guys, especially the shooter, they'll let you go."

"I don't know those guys. I was not there."

"You know son, I have known Scotty for a longtime and he said you were one of them."

"Mr. Scotty, I don't believe you."

"Are you calling me a liar, boy?"

"No, sir," Jordan said looking him in the eyes.

"I can't help you if you don't cooperate with me."

"Then I guess I have to get me another lawyer."

"I am doing this practically for free. If you think you can find you someone else within the next two hours then good luck," he turned and left the room.

Jordan was alone when the officer brought him before the judge. Joseph got up and walked toward the front of the courtroom. An officer came up to him to keep him from going any further. He told the officer that he was the boy's father. The officer allowed him to proceed.

"Where is your attorney?" Joseph whispered in his son's ear.

"He wants me to say I did this," Jordan said choking back the tears.

Joseph looked at his son with compassion, not knowing what to say.

"I didn't do it."

"You don't have to say that to me son. I know you didn't do it. We are going to prove it," Joseph said not taking his eyes off the boy.

Joseph reached in his pocket and handed him a note that Layla had written.

"Ma-Me wanted me to give this to you," he said.

They both looked at the picture on the note. It appeared to be

I Blew God a Kiss

a picture of Layla hugging Jordan. It read, "Welcome Home!" They looked at each other and started laughing.

"Ma-Me needs to work on her drawings if she's going to make it as a fashion designer," Jordan said still laughing.

When the judge called for Jordan, Joseph went up with him. Sadie, Juanita and Sam were sitting close to the back. The courtroom was crowded that morning and the judge wasn't in a good mood.

"Please God, let him be good to my boy," Sadie whispered.

Juanita held Sadie's hand tightly. Sam didn't say a word. Sam was there the night that Jordan was born. The connection he felt for Jordan was more than an uncle, it was a paternal one.

Jordan was nervous especially after what the lawyer had said about Mr. Scotty. He knew that Mr. Scotty was upset about him quitting his job, but surely he wouldn't go this far.

"Jordan D'Wayne Porter," the judge called.

"Yes sir," Jordan responded.

"And who are you?"

"I am Joseph Porter, Your honor, his father."

"Well Mr. Porter it seems that your boy has gotten himself in some trouble here."

"Your honor he is innocent."

"Were you with him when this terrible tragedy happened?"

"No, Sir but I know my son."

"Mr. Porter we would all like to think that our children wouldn't do any harm. I must hold him over for trial. We have a witness saying that your son was there. The date for the hearing is August 22nd."

"Sir—what about the bond?"

"I am sorry Mr. Porter I can't allow a bond in a matter of this nature. Your son is being charged with arm robbery and attempted murder. There is no bond." The judge hit his gavel on the desk and called his next case.

Joseph returned home with his family. He sat on the back porch with Sam. He was stunned. He could not believe what the judge said.

"This is more serious than I thought," he said to Sam.

"You know what we need to do. You know who can help us," Sam said.

"No way, man! You know that Sadie wouldn't agree to that."

"Joe, Sadie would sell her soul to get Jay Pee out of jail."

"Yeah, but Vicky?" Joseph said shaking his head vehemently, "and what about Ma-Me?"

"Look man," Sam said putting his hand on Joseph's shoulder, "I told you years ago that you need to start preparing Ma-Me to meet her biological mother. She is wondering about that now, but she's afraid to ask you. Victoria has always been pragmatic she will not stand for what they are doing to Jay."

Joseph took a deep sigh. He understood what Sam was saying and he knew that Victoria would not allow Jordan to spend another night in jail. He had to find the right time to approach Sadie.

Sadie had not forgiven him for the affair and she refuse to forgive Victoria for giving up a child like Layla. Sadie raised her as her own daughter even though she looked nearly white. Sadie's story to those who asked had been that her great-grandmother was part white and that Layla got her complexion from her. Nobody believed Sadie. Everyone knew Joseph had a reputation with the ladies, and

I Blew God a Kiss

since Layla just appeared one day kept them speculating on who the real mother could be.

Joseph decided to talk with Nanmu. He realized that if there was any hope in getting Sadie to allow Victoria to help Jordan that he needed Nanmu's support. He decided to sleep on it and wait until the next day to talk to Nanmu. Sam agreed. It was late in the evening and they could do nothing until morning so Sam said goodnight.

Nanmu knew that for Joseph to come to her he had to be desperate. She could see the pain in his face so she left out her usual lectures. She waited until Joseph had finished speaking before she said anything.

"Joe if you think there's a chance that Vicky can get Jay Pee out of jail then I'd say call her. Right now! But we both know that it's a little more complicated than that. What will Sadie think? We just had some words about that. I think we should let Jay Pee decide. After all this is his life we are talking about. He's the one that will be best equipped to handle Ma-Me. She worships that child. However difficult this would be for her he would be able to help her through it. I will go see Jay Pee," she said moving toward the closet to get her hat.

"Are you working today?"

"No Mam. I took the week off," he said.

"Alright, I'll stop by the house after I get back. Just drop me off and I'll take a cab back."

"Nanmu, you don't need to take a cab. I can wait for you."

"No, I don't want Sadie to know that you came to me; it would be easier if she thought this was my idea."

Jordan was transferred to the county jail since it would be

three weeks until his trial. Nanmu didn't like the guard searching her things and she said so. He told her that it was procedure. The guard led her to a small room where she waited for them to bring Jordan to see her. Her heart broke when she saw his face. She cleared her throat and asked him how he was doing. He didn't respond. He dropped his head. Jordan normally had a positive disposition and a talent for cheering others when times were bad.

Nanmu tried again this time, reaching across the table to touch his hand. The security guard that was standing behind Jordan moved forward and Nanmu pulled her hand away.

"Wouldn't we do for a pan of my cornbread fresh out of the oven covered with butter?"

Jordan looked up and gave her a smile.

"That's my boy. You have such a great smile it is a shame to waste it with a frown."

"It's hard Nanmu," was all he was able to get out when his eyes watered with tears. He dropped his head again.

"Look at me child."

Nanmu had three different voices. The, I am Nanmu, I mean business voice. The Nanmu, I want you to learn this, voice. The Nanmu, I love you voice. This voice to Jordan sounded like a combination of all three. One he had never heard before.

He looked into her eyes. Nanmu had big beautiful brown calm and peaceful eyes.

"I know that I don't know what you're going through. You will not hear those words from me. I can and I am praying for our Lord to give you the strength and protection that you will need while in this place. Do you believe that he can do that for you?"

I Blew God a Kiss

"It's hard Nanmu. I don't know if I can."

"I know this is hard honey, but you must try."

"I will."

"Listen your dad told me about that horrible experience that you had with that Mr. Cane."

"I can't believe that Mr. Scotty would say those things about me."

"It doesn't matter. We will get you out of this."

"I need a lawyer Nanmu, a good one."

"That's why I'm here. Your dad sent me."

"Why?"

"He wants to see if we can get Mrs. Vicky."

"Mrs. Victoria, what about Ma-Me?"

"That's why the decision must be yours."

"I don't know Nanmu I want to get out but not if Ma-Me's gonna get hurt."

"You will be able to help Ma-Me if it comes to that."

"What about mama? She won't allow it. You know how she feels about Mrs. Victoria."

"I think she will do whatever needs to be done to get you out. You let us know and we will support your decision?"

She started to leave and asked the officer if she could give him a hug. He said that she could.

I Blew God a Kiss

Layla was conceived during the time when Elvis ruled and James Brown jammed to *"Please, Please, Please."* Victoria Lynn Jospin was the daughter of one of the richest men in the small cotton mill town where the Porters lived. She was home on summer vacation when she first took notice of Joseph. He was a foreman at one of her father's plants. Her father owned six plants within a fifty-mile radius. He owned some others throughout the southern states. Victoria had a younger sister. Her dad hoped for a son that could take over the family business, but that never happened. The trip to the plant that day was the second time that Victoria had been there. She was only twelve years old the first time.

Joseph was standing behind his desk with a clipboard in his hand, talking to one of the workers. Victoria dressed elegantly. She wore a pale green dress that brought out her large beautiful hazel eyes. She was flirtatious with the workers. So Joseph didn't think anything of it when she came on to him. Joseph liked women but he wanted to be the one who made the move. He told himself, man you would get hung if you even looked at this girl the wrong way. A page came over the intercom for her father that called him upstairs. He asked Victoria to come with him.

"No sir," she said to him, "I would like to know about what they do on this level. Can you ask Mr. Porter to show me around?"

"Vicky I don't want to leave you here alone," he said.

"I am a big girl daddy, besides I am not alone," she said looking lustfully at Joseph.

"Okay, I won't be long," he gave her a kiss on the mouth.

She took a leisurely gait toward Joseph and set on the edge of the desk. She pulled her dress up slightly.

He gave her a slow inviting look from her ankles to the top of where she pulled up her dress.

"Down girl," he said.

"Why?"

"I am a married man."

"I'm not."

"You're not what?"

"A married anything."

He laughed, enticed and amused.

Joseph spent the summer hanging out with Victoria. It was mostly at her demands. Even though he enjoyed the time with her, he was afraid that her father would find out. She tried to assure him that she could handle her father.

"I don't know what type of men you have dealt with, but I am a black man with a white man's little girl."

She would just kiss him and tell him not to worry about it.

When Victoria returned to school he only heard from her once and that was to tell him to meet her. The meeting turned out to be a shocker. He never knew that she was pregnant. Layla was

I Blew God a Kiss

a week old when Victoria brought her to Joseph. Even though she had no marks of a black child Victoria couldn't take the chance of her father finding out. She knew that Joseph was right. Her father wouldn't fire him; he would kill him and disown her.

Joseph took Jordan to the lake with him the day he met with Victoria. He was nervous and didn't want to handle the encounter alone. Victoria didn't say much to him she cried and kissed Layla good-bye.

He told Jordan to stay close to him when they took the baby to Sadie. Jordan and Sadie had a special relationship. Even he didn't understand. Joseph always tried to get Sadie to stop being so soft on Jordan.

She would say to him, "He's my baby and he will always be my baby."

"Making a baby into a man will never happen with the way you treat him," Joseph would say.

Sadie would respond, "Making him a man is your job—not mine."

Something broke inside Sadie the day Layla came. It was as if all the dreams Sadie had for her family diminished. She felt as though she would never trust Joseph again. Months went by before she could even allow Joseph to touch her. She barely ate or slept. Before she drank beer and wine coolers, but the devastation of the infidelity turned her to hard liquor.

I Blew God a Kiss

When Layla found out that Mr. Scotty had lied on Jordan she desperately felt a need to intervene for the brother she loved so completely. She resolved in her heart to confront Mr. Scotty. She headed up the road toward the A&P with a stone face and the courage of a lion. She was so intently focused that she didn't notice someone following her. She turned quickly. It was Buster.

"Buster—what you doing? You go back home. Yo' mama gone kill you."

"Where you goin Ma-Me?"

"That mean old Mr. Scotty is telling lies on Jay Pee and I'm gone tell him to stop."

"You can't do that Ma-Me. What if he do somein' to you?"

She pulled him by the arm and starting walking him back down the street.

"Listen to me Buster, you go home. Yo' mama will be worryin' bout' you."

Buster was a couple years younger than Layla. Buster did not go to school because of a heart condition. His mom was protective of him and would not allow him to play with the other kids. Layla persuaded Nanmu to talk his mother into letting her spend time with him. They had been friends for two years. Layla would bring home her school lessons and teach Buster what she learned. Buster was a good student and eager to learn. His smile could melt a rainbow and his energy for life could ignite a flame in an ice bucket.

He stopped in his tracks. He did not want Layla to walk him home.

"No, Ma-Me, I'm goin' wit' you, please don't make me go back. I don't have no fun," he said flashing Lalya the most incredible smile.

"Oh alright, but you not goin' in with me. I talk to him by myself."

They walked about four more blocks laughing and talking all the way. Layla enjoyed being with Buster. He was the only person outside of her family who never made comments about her complexion.

Layla walked into the A&P the ferocious lion that started out with her had turned into a frighten kitten. Her legs were cemented to the floor and she could hear her heart beat in her ears. She saw Mr. Scotty walking down one of the aisles. She walked over to the service desk and asked if she could see Mr. Scotty. The woman behind the desk called him over the speaker. He came right away.

"Yes, what can I do for you young lady?" He asked her in a voice friendlier than Lalya expected.

"I need to talk to you about my brother."

"Your brother? I see. Come into my office," he said.

She followed him into a room that was behind the service

desk.

Layla looked around at all the clutter and she stopped right inside the door.

He turned and said, "What do you have to say to me?" Layla couldn't speak. "Say on chile. Don't waste my time," the friendly voice was no longer there.

"I want you to tell the judge it wasn't my brother who robbed you."

He laughed an unruly laugh. He walked up to her and started stroking her hair.

"And what you doing for me if I do you this favor?"

Layla backed away getting closer to the door.

"What you doing with them colored people anyway a white girl like you?"

"Thems my family."

"They are not your family. You think that black woman bore you? What lies they been feeding you."

"You the one who's a lie. You lied on Jay Pee."

"Well you can fix that just come sit on Mr. Scotty's lap. It will be our secret."

Layla turned and ran out the door. She could hear Mr. Scotty laughing behind her.

When she got outside to Buster she was shaking and crying.

"What that man do to you?" Buster asked.

"Let's go," she said.

Buster didn't say anything. He followed her waiting until she was calm enough to talk.

"That's a nasty man. He is mean and nasty."

"He hurt you Ma-Me?

"No he made me mad. He wanted me to sit on his lap."

"Ma-Me you need to tell."

"I can't—don't you tell neither, Buster."

Buster's mom was walking toward them. Buster looked up at Layla and smiled. His mom didn't say a word; she didn't speak when Layla said hello to her. His mom walked beside them in silence. When they got to where Buster lived, he waved good-bye to Layla. She watched them as they went into the house. She didn't know that would be the last time she would see him. Buster died three weeks later. She did not know his real name until he died. His name was John Lewis Avers.

L ayla was 17 when she found out about her biological mother. She woke in the middle of the night to what was the most violent fight that her parents ever had. David and Juanita were standing outside their room. Layla told them not to worry and go back to bed. She stood in the hall unnoticed. The shouts were fierce. Her father was holding Sadie trying to wrestle her down.

"Please Sadie calm down. We have to talk about this."

"No we don't and no we won't! I will not allow Ma-Me to have anything to do with that woman!"

"Sadie, she just want to spend some time with her."

"Not if I can help it she won't. She gave that chile away like she was one of her used sports cars. Ma-Me wasn't good enough for her then and she won't be now. Get your hands off me," she shouted as she tried to untangle herself from his hold.

"Sadie please!"

"You promised me that she would not interfere in our lives, she waits until the chile is grown and now she wants to play mama!"

"Sadie, Ma-Me will be a woman soon, and I think she should

be allowed to make that choice."

"You think! You think! Did I have a choice? Did Ma-Me have a choice? You selfish bastard. You go out whenever you get ready to satisfy that thang between your legs, not caring what it does to me or this family. For years I have stood by and let you do what you wanted to do. And you, you brought her here for Jay Pee's trial and I looked the other way—"

Layla did not hear another word; she felt as if she got stung by a giant wasp. She could not move. She could not breathe. The hall slowly enclosed around her. She felt as if she was in a narrow tube. Everything went dark. The only light she could see was the light that radiated around her shaking hands. At that moment Joseph looked up and saw Layla. The argument was so intense, they never realized that she was there.

Layla turned around and went to her room and Joseph followed her. Layla could not say a word. She picked up her suitcase; it was an expensive suitcase that she got on her 16th birthday. She realized now that it was probably from Mrs. Victoria. She did not see or hear Joseph. It was as if he were not there. She had no form or order in the way she was packing. She snatched her clothes by the bundle and stuffed them in. She tossed jewelry and make-up. Tears and mucous were running down here check and into her mouth.

Still in her pajamas she picked up the bundled up mess of a suitcase and headed for the door. She had no direction where she was going. She only knew that she could not stay there.

Joseph tried to block her way. When he saw the hurt and the anger in her eyes, he let her go. He tried to ask where she was going. She didn't hear him. Juanita came out of the room just as Layla was passing her door.

"Ma-Me, where you going? Ma-Me, where you going? Ma-Me, where you going? Ma-Me, you coming back?"

Sadie blocked the front door and wouldn't let her pass.

"Ma-Me, you are not leaving this house," she said

Layla turned around and headed for the back door. Sadie started to go behind her and Joseph stopped her. Sadie's knees hit the floor and she cried.

"How are we going to fix this mess?" Sadie asked.

Joseph knew that Laya wouldn't go far from the house especially at night. He looked out the window and sure enough she was sitting on the old swing. He sent Sadie to bed and stayed awake hoping that Layla would come in the house.

The morning brought clarity to Layla and she went to her friend, Lee. Lee Sims was coolness when coolness was hot. He had a smooth Afro, with never a hair out of place. He took pride in the way he dressed. His shoes were spit shine to perfection. He had a gap between his two front teeth. It wasn't a flaw; it gave him a certain appeal that he wasn't insecure about. His eyes were radiant when he smiled and let off a slight twinkle. His skin was dark and beautiful. He didn't hang around guys in the neighborhood and most of the women thought he was gay because he didn't come on to them.

That's why he and Layla became friends. She spent most of high school alienated by the black students. They thought because of her beauty, she had to be stuck-up. They never gave her a chance to prove otherwise. Most of the white students didn't want anything to do with her because she lived with a black family. The students who tried to reach out to her she shunned them mistrusting their motives.

Layla relayed to Lee all the horrific details of her parents' fight. She told him that she was not going back. Lee didn't think she was making a clear or wise choice, that she was allowing her anger to control her.

"Look, Ma-Me—" he started.

"Layla, my name is Layla," she shouted! "I don't know why they gave me that stupid name anyway."

"I thought you liked being called Ma-Me."

"I did when I was little, not anymore."

"Okay, Layla you have one more year of school. What do you plan to do just drop out?"

"You dropped out and you turned out okay."

"I got my GED and then went on to college."

"So I can do the same."

Lee looked at her, how beautiful and innocent. He knew he was fighting a losing battle.

"Ma-Me—sorry, I have called you Ma-Me all your life; give me a little more time to stop calling you that. Where do you plan to go?"

"New York."

"No, oh no. That city will eat you alive. Why New York? You've never been to New York?"

"No but Jay Pee has taken me there plenty of times."

"Layla, New York is not like some game you play on your porch swing."

"Well, Jay Pee is there and she's there."

"Who?"

"You know, my other mother, the real one."

"So what do you think she is going to do, take you into her princess lily white world and welcome you, a black kid from Alabama."

"Well, I look white besides, she accepted Jay Pee."

"That's different, Jay Pee's her apprentice. You talkin' bout being her daughter, and looking white, is not being white."

Lee's statement upset Layla. She started getting her things without saying a word.

Lee stepped in front of her and said, "Ma-Me, I am sorry I didn't mean that. I love you Ma-Me. You can stay here with me forever."

"Do you mean that?"

"Yes, I do," he said getting a little closer to her.

"Do you really love me?"

"Ma-Me!" He kissed her softly on the lips.

S adie was furious the next morning when she awoke and
Layla wasn't in her room. She kicked, banged, and
threw everything that was in her way. Juanita and David were afraid
to come out of their rooms. David finally convinced Juanita to get
them something to eat and drink. He tried to convince Juanita to call
Nanmu but she wasn't hearing that.

Sadie began packing Joseph's clothes. All the while swearing
and picking up an object once in a while to throw at him.

"Sadie what are you doing?"

"You are getting out of my house."

"Your house? The last time I checked I was the one paying
bills in this house."

"I will not even justify that with an answer. You are getting
up out of here," she shouted. "Out, Out, take this stuff and get out,"
she threw a shirt to his belly.

Joseph did the only thing he knew to do. He picked up his
bags and left. When Joseph left Sadie went into the living room and
sat on the sofa. She did not know where all the tears were coming
from. She simply could not stop crying. Once the noise quieted
down, Juanita and David came and sat beside her. Neither of them

said a word. After Sadie stopped crying she asked them if they remembered the last time the family was all together.

"Yes mam they said in unison."

"Jay Pee was funny," David said.

"Ma-Me and me were playing cards. I beat her the way I always did. That was six years ago right before Jay Pee left for college, my how time fly's." Sadie said with a smirk on her face.

"Jay Pee was telling the knock, knock jokes," Juanita said.

"Yeah the silly ones," David laughed.

Juanita started, "Knock, knock."

"Who's there?" Sadie and Davie asked.

"Henry."

"Henry who," they both chimed.

"Hen-wry having for dinner."

They all laughed.

"Oh, oh," said Sadie, "I am gone tell yall a funny one."

"Mama don't mess up the punch line," Nita said, still laughing at the knock, knock joke.

"Who me? I never mess up the punch line, okay here it goes, "What do you call a dog with three legs?"

"What, what?"

"Nobody," she said, "he won't come anyway."

"That ain't right," Davie said.

"That ain't the way Jay Pee tell it," Nita piped in.

"Well I am not a comedy teller like Jay Pee. I am a mother who is about to put Henry on for dinner."

I Blew God a Kiss

Layla's first night away from her family gave her a sense of emptiness that she had not experienced. Lee was up early and had an omelet made for her which she declined to eat. Lee didn't have a job like regular people. Layla never understood how he could afford his jazzy apartment. It was fancy throughout. Lee's album collection was phenomenal. He had everything from Muddy Waters, Nat King Cole, Charlie Parker, Miles Davis, Nina Simone and so many they couldn't be listened to in a lifetime.

His knowledge of music amazed Layla. He would take her backstage to the Jazz and Blues concerts. He said they paid him to go to the concerts and write about what he thought about the music. Layla never believed him. She thought who would be dumb enough to let you go to a free show and then give you money to say what you thought. Anyway she went when he invited her.

Lee called Nanmu to let her know that Layla was with him. He asked her to give him a chance to tell Layla he called her. Layla didn't mind him calling Nanmu. She just wished that he would have allowed her to decide.

He pleaded with her to eat or at the least to drink some juice.

She wouldn't. He didn't force her out of bed. He could tell she didn't have the strength. Lee tried everything that he could to get Layla out of bed. His favorite saying was when you come to the end of your rope, tie a knot. He dressed up in a black tuxedo with a purple cummerbund. He stood outside the door and started singing.

"I woke up this morning and I was in an awful mood—I was broke and hungry and I didn't know what to do—It's a terrible little thang when you'll in this world alone—When you don't have no friends and no place to call your own—So tied I can cry, I can lay right down and die—Won't somebody tell me baby—Please tell me the reason why." He sang the words repeating them in a slow soulful tone giving a perfect rendition of T-Bone Walker.

Layla started laughing so hard that she fell out of bed.

"Well," he said, "I give you my best performance and what do you do. You laugh."

Layla held onto his leg and pulled him to the floor. She laid her head in his lap.

"Ma-Me you are too beautiful to be so unhappy."

She didn't say anything.

"What are you going to do?"

She kissed his hand and said, "Lee, can you run me a bath?"

"That's my girl, you got it."

When Sadie put Joseph out he went to Sam. He thought it was best to allow Sadie to cool off. She told him to leave before, but she had never packed his clothes.

"Man, you got anything in this house to drink?" Joseph said as soon as Sam opened the door.

I Blew God a Kiss

"What's up man? You look like you just got your face kicked in."

"Ma-Me's gone."

"What you say?"

"Ma-Me overheard Sadie and me fight about Vicky."

"Oh, man. I knew this would happen."

"Knock it off man. I don't—"

"Well, who came to who here?"

"Sadie put me out."

Sam started laughing, hard.

"Man, I come for help and you laugh."

"Well, when have you left home because Sadie told you?"

"What you got in this house to drink."

"I made some kool-aid earlier."

"You kiddin me, right!"

"No, man I'm not kidding you. This isn't a liquor store."

"Fo' get you man."

"Where did she go?

"What?"

"Ma-Me, do you know where she would go?"

"I never seen my little girl hurt like that," Joseph wept.

Sam went to the phone and called his neighbor to see if he had anything to drink. He said he had some gin. Sam asked him to bring it over.

Sam didn't say anything else. He didn't know what to say. He prayed that wherever she went, she was safe. There was a rapid knock at the door.

"Hey man," his friend began, "when did you…" he stopped talking when he saw Joseph.

"If you need anything else man let me know," he said

"Thanks man," Sam replied.

Sam went into the kitchen and got two glasses and the pitcher of kool-aid. He poured a glass for Joseph and a nearly full glass of kool-aid for himself, flavored with a little bit of gin.

Joseph shook his head and took a drink.

Sam took a sip of his glass and gagged as if he had drunk poison.

"Hey man, you don't have to do this," Joseph said.

"No, man I'm cool," Sam said choking.

Joseph stood up and started pacing the floor. He hit his fist into his hand.

"I should go over there and kick Sadie's butt all over that house."

"Cool out man, that's my sister you're talking about."

"I know—that's why I am here," he smiled and sat back down.

"Joe you know Ma-Me is a good kid. She has a strong bond with the family."

"I am hoping that she will go to Nanmu."

"She is hurting right now. Does she have a friend she would go to?"

"No, Ma-Me doesn't have many friends. She goes to concerts with that Lee fellow sometimes. I don't know, maybe Jay Pee, she misses him."

"She'll be back as soon as she's had a chance to heal. We all have to deal with pain and hurt it's a part of life. Once she's had a chance to heal she'll be back. Maybe you should get an arbitrator," he said.

"A what, man, that gin is going to your head. Why you always got to use this psycho analyzing stuff? Can't you stop being a counselor for one minute?"

"Hey man, she's my blood—"

They both started yelling at each other their words became babble. Finally Sam felt as if he were being over powered so he stopped talking.

"Do you have some kind of psych book under your pillow or something? Geez can you just talk without having to analyze a situation."

"Well, excuse me for breathing," Sam said with an attitude.

"I want to know, tell me where you get this stuff? You have an answer for everything. All I want to know is where does it come from?"

Sam was silent for a few minutes. Then he said with a muffled voice, Dr. Ruth."

"Man, you are full of it," Joseph spit back.

I Blew God a Kiss

The imagination is a powerful force. What if you can live two lives, one with the eyes of imagination, the other with the eyes of reality?

Grassy Creek, Alabama was a small town. Maybe calling it a town is an understatement. Grassy Creek was once a plantation. When President Lincoln signed the Emancipation Proclamation, the white families in Grassy Creek continued to keep their slaves. Nobody fought to change things. They did not know how. It was when Dr. Martin Luther King, Jr. gave a speech that reached into the hearts of the nations that allowed even the people in the smallest of places to dream. People began to have hope for their lives and for the lives of their children.

It was Layla's destination to put Grassy Creek on the map. She spent three days with Lee when it finally clicked that she had a dream to fulfill. She wanted to face Joseph, but she was still angry. Whenever she thought about it, her throat blazed like fire.

"Miss Mary Mack, Mack, Mack—All Dressed in Black, Black, Black—With Silver Buttons, Buttons, Buttons—All Down Her Back, Back, Back."

She could hear some kids giggling. The sounds of their rhythmic hands clapping together lifted her heart and soul as she sat on the front steps of Lee's apartment. She said a prayer and asked God to always remind her of this time of peace. Peace that she could always look back on when times got hard. She was finally ready to leave, so she went back inside to tell Lee.

Lee once again urged her to call Joseph. She said that she would call him when she got to New York.

"New York! Layla please change your mind."

"Thanks a lot my friend," she said sarcastically.

"I am your friend and I would do anything to stop you from making the worst mistake of your life."

"So does that mean that you're not giving me the money?"

"Ma-Me, I am giving you the money because I know that once you get something in that little noggin," he said knocking on her head, "you won't let it go."

Lee went into the bedroom and came out with ten crisp one hundred dollar bills.

When he started to give her the money, he said, "I know you only asked for five hundred but that won't take you far in New York."

When she reached for the money, he pulled it away from her.

"You promise me you will call Jay Pee as soon as you get there."

Again she reached for it and again he snatched it back.

"Promise me that no matter what happens you won't take a cab when you get off the bus you'll call Jay Pee."

Layla asked Lee to give her a minute alone so she could call Nanmu.

I Blew God a Kiss

Layla's first couple of nights in New York was a nightmare. I want to roll back the darkness. I feel there are spears piercing at my soul. People, masses of people, please go away. New York was nothing like Jordan's porch swing trips. She thought.

The masses of people suffocated Layla. She could not believe there could be so many people in such a small area. Fear overwhelmed her. Everything that Lee had said about New York was true. She wanted to go home but her pride would not allow it. She had to come up with a plan or this city would destroy her. She wanted to call Jordan, but she felt betrayed by him as well.

"I can't believe he knew about Vicky and didn't tell me," she said with tears in her eyes, "I can't stay in this motel," she looked in the mirror which distorted her face because of the multiple cracks.

"I can be white. All I have to do is dye my hair blond. It would be easier for me to get modeling jobs. I need to find a photographer. Lee was right, this money won't last long.

"Dear God, I am so afraid. Please protect me. Show me what to do and where to go. I feel so alone," she prayed.

The next morning she took one hundred and fifty dollars to the beauty salon. Nia Sun a lovely slender Japanese young woman was her hairstylist. Layla liked Nia right away.

"Why you want change your hair culor hon', this culor look great on you."

"I just need a change. You think you can straighten it for me too."

"Sure hon', what ever. You need haircut. I have style for you. Look real nice," she said with a smile.

"No I like it long, maybe just a trim."

They talked for awhile about hairstyles and different color blonds. Layla didn't realize there were so many choices.

When she left the salon Nia had given her more than a new look but a confidence that she had never felt. Nia called a close friend of her family's, who was looking for someone to work in his store. She told Layla that this would be perfect for her since he was offering a small room with the job.

S he arrived on the ten-thirty bus, took a taxis to this little motel. She spent a couple of nights there. This morning she went to this salon. She came out with a new look," Frankie said, laying the pictures before Jordan.

"My little sister is a white girl," Jordan said shaking his head.

"And one good-looking mama," Frankie said with a grin.

"She checked out of the motel and took a room above this little store. The owner's name is Raymond Kerr. He is a widow sixty or so. I think he might be Hungarian. People say he's decent. I think he really wants to help her."

"Listen man, I know I didn't hire you to look after my little sister but can you keep an eye on her for the rest of the week. I don't want anything to happen to her."

"Then what, after the week?"

"I don't know. Maybe she'll be ready to talk," he paused, "keep an eye on her okay."

"You got it man. She's in good hands," Frankie said with confidence.

I Blew God a Kiss

Frankie Petro worked for Jordan at Victoria's Law firm. He had been his investigator for a year. He was twenty-five and dropped out of college with only a semester left to finish his degree. He came from a wealthy family with a hard to please father. This job at Victoria's firm was more to get back at his dad, but he had come to love the thrill of being a spy and catching bad guys. A handsome Italian with a beautiful accent, he was a hit with the ladies but committed to none.

Jordan decided it was time to have a talk with Victoria. He called and set up a lunch date with her.

"Jordan, you've been with me for four years and you have never called to buy me lunch. You are free to say whatever you want except you're quitting. You are the best paralegal I have."

"Mrs. Vicky."

"I know this is serious. You haven't called me Mrs. in years. What is it Jordan?"

He reached into his pocket and pulled out the pictures that Frankie had taken. He laid them on the table in front of her without saying a word. She picked up the pictures and started flipping quickly through them.

"Who is this? Does it have anything to do with a case?"

"It's Ma-Me," he said.

"Ma-Me is here in New York. What is she doing here? Who's with her?"

The waitress came to the table and asked if they were ready to order. Vicky ordered a scotch. Jordan shook his head no.

"About a week ago," he started, "Ma-Me overheard Mama and Pop fighting. She knows you're her mother. She's not talking to anybody except Nanmu and she's not listening to her. Her friend Lee called me and told me she was coming. I hope you don't mind I asked Frankie to keep an eye on her. Right now she is angry with me too. She said she never wanted to talk to me again."

"She doesn't mean that Jordan. You know how much she loves you. Where is she now? I'm going to see her."

"You can't. I know Ma-Me. If you force her, she'll shut you out completely."

The waitress came back to the table. Jordan ordered the soup of the day and Vicky ordered a Greek salad.

"Then what do we do—nothing?"

"For now, she will realize she can't make it out here on her on. I want her to come to us."

"And if she doesn't?"

"She will."

"I don't know if I want to take that chance. We have to get her off the streets. You know what kind of predators are out there."

"She is smart she won't get suckered into doing anything she doesn't want to do."

"Okay, you keep her watched. I don't care what it cost. Hire someone to help Frankie," Jordan shook his head.

"Have you talked to Joseph?"

"No."

"Jordan, I know you haven't forgiven Joseph but he is a good man. You need to call him."

"I will when I get back to the office," he said.

Layla agreed to work for Mr. Kerr for room and board. It

was not much of a room. It was a small space that Mr. Kerr used for storage. He cleared it out for her and set up a small bed and night table. He liked having her around. It had been a longtime since anyone lived with him. He had a good-natured, kindly spirit, which created in her a feeling of safety and security

"Whaz you running vay from child," he inquired of Layla.

"I heard New York is the place to be that's all."

"Dunt you got family who worr-ry for chu."

"No sir, there's no one," she said.

He observed the sadness in her eyes and knew that she was lying.

"I have daughter and grandson. I vary proud papa. I sho' you pictures. You rest now."

Layla sat on the bed removing the card Nia had given her. She considered calling her, but she resolved to give it a little more thought.

Layla worked in the store for a few days and decided to go see Harold Long, the photographer that Nia recommended.

I have some ideas on the shots I want," she commanded of him after he tried to push her into taking the pictures his way.

He looked over some of the sample pictures she gave him.

"What jobs are you looking to get," he said tossing the photos aside.

"I would like to do some fashion magazines, maybe some runway."

"That's a competitive area. Have any experience with that stuff? In this city you need someone to vouch for you."

"My look can vouch for me."

"You know honey, you are fresh and hot but this is New York. Every fresh new hotty comes to this city."

"Listen, just take the pictures and let's see what happens," Layla snapped.

"Sweetie you don't need to get angry. I am here to help you. You need to show a little skin; you want to be a model, you shouldn't have a problem with getting undressed, that's where the money is," he said

Layla gathered her belongings and headed for the door.

"Wait a minute," Harold said, "If you got a problem with that, we will do it your way. You're the boss."

"Well I do have a problem with it. Obviously I made a mistake by coming here."

"No you didn't. Forgive me. I'll shoot the pictures you want."

Frankie called Jordan and gave him the report that Layla was with Harold Long.

"Who is Harold Long?" Jordan asked.

"He is a scum porn photographer," Frankie remarked.

Jordan was silent.

"You want me to go in there and get her?"

"No."

"What do you want me to do man?"

"Nothing," he answered.

"Why am I watching her—if I can't do anything?" Frankie was upset with Jordan's inert response.

"Gotti, I am pulling you off my sister. I am sorry I asked you to do this. Come on in man."

I Blew God a Kiss

"What do you mean?"

"Trust me, come in."

I Blew God a Kiss

Layla called Nia furious that she had sent her to Harold. "Calm down Layla. Harold is a good photographer."

"He kept trying to get me to take my clothes off."

Nia laughed.

"Oh you think that is funny!" Layla was furious.

"No, that Harold. He take his mama's picture butt naked if she let."

"I have never been so humiliated. You could have at least warned me."

"Let me make up to you. There's party this weekend. Go with me."

"I don't think so," she said pouting.

"Come on, you meet people. It get you job. Pick you up Saturday night at eight."

She agreed but the churning feeling in her stomach was screaming big mistake.

Layla was down to her last hundred. Mr. Kerr was providing her with free room plus meals but she needed to find work soon. Once she calmed down she thought that the party could be a positive experience.

Nia arrived on time and was shocked to see Layla looking

like a Barbie doll.

"You's gonna knock'em out," Nia gave her a kiss on the lips.

Layla felt a little uncomfortable.

"If you's givin' kiss give kiss," Nia said.

Layla didn't say anything.

Nia was talkative on the drive to the party. She laid down some ground rules for Layla, since this was her first New York party. She assured her there would be plenty of contacts within the fashion industry. She asked Layla if she knew anything about cocaine. Layla told her that she heard of it but never used it. Nia said that it would be a lot of people offering it to her. She told her to take it from them but give it to her.

"If you don't, they think you's Five-O," she said.

"What if they want me to do some there?"

"You tell you had hit."

Nia showed Layla off like she was a brand-new trophy. She knew everybody. She was knowledgeable about who had money and who didn't. She knew who had no money but had connections. She introduced Layla to Marilyn Coachett a prestigious Greek fashion designer.

She had long brown hair and the most beautiful white teeth that Layla had ever seen. The outfit she wore did not compliment her though. Layla thought. She had on a green and yellow sheer blouse with ruffle sleeves and a pleated mini skirt. If she's a successful designer, then I am headed for the right career. She needs my help.

"Layla, what a pretty name—for a pretty lady," Marilyn said as she combed Layla's hair with her fingers.

Thank you," Layla responded.

I Blew God a Kiss

"How old are you Darling?"

"Nineteen."

"You don't look a day over fifteen."

Layla blushed.

"Its okay darling. You have a fresh look. That's what I am looking for. How would you like to model some of my designs?"

"Wow—"

"I pay well, one hundred-fifty dollars an hour. I will also pay to train you. I work with one of the top modeling schools in New York. What do you say?"

"I say, when do I start," Layla said laughing.

"This is the number to La Dea's modeling school," she said handing her a business card, "call her and see when you can start. She'll let me know when you're ready."

"I don't know what to say. Thank you."

Marilyn dashed away to talk to someone else, leaving Layla standing there.

Layla was so excited she could hardly stand still. She looked around the room for Nia, but she didn't see her. The party was going on in four different rooms. She searched every room but didn't see Nia.

Layla felt as if someone's eyes were watching her. She was a bit paranoid since she didn't know anybody. She looked around the kitchen where she was standing but didn't notice anybody. She turned around quickly and knocked a drink out of someone's hand.

"I am sorry, I didn't see you," she said.

"Oh you can ruin my suit anytime man," he said.

"I'll get something to clean that up for you."

"Don't bother it'll dry. What's your name?"

"Layla."

"Just Layla like Cher."

"No," she said giggling, "Layla Porter."

"Well Layla Porter would you like to dance."

"I didn't see a dance floor anywhere."

He grabbed her hand and escorted her to the basement. It was a huge smoke-filled room with strobe lights that gave it a slight glimmer. In the corner she saw Nia wrapped up with a guy. He had his hands under her dress. She decided not to interrupt. A slow song started to play and they danced.

"So what's your name?"

"Reggie."

"Just Reggie like just Sonny."

"Ha-ha, you catch on man and you are cute. How old are you?"

"Nineteen," she said.

Nia came over and tapped her on the shoulder.

"Let's go," she said. She looked angry.

Layla thanked Reggie for the dance and followed Nia out.

Nia didn't say a word on the drive home. Finally Layla broke the silence.

"Who was that guy you were kissing?"

"Don't know," she said with a whisper.

"You were kissing some dude and you don't know his name?"

"He had cute butt."

Layla threw her hands in the air and said, "oh, brother."

I Blew God a Kiss

"You's not my mother!" Nia said yelling.

"That's you," Layla turned her head and gazed out the window.

"You's got nerve, judging me. You need concern with loser you dance with."

"That's why we left?"

"I try saving your ungrateful butt."

"Thanks."

"Get out my car," Nia said as she approached her building.

Layla reached over and kissed her on the lips. Nia smiled.

It was a relief for Layla to be back in her room. What a night she thought. She reached in her pocket and pulled out the coke Reggie had slipped her. She forgot to give it to Nia. She looked at the card for La Dea's, "I didn't tell Nia about my job offer," she said hitting her fist on her forehead. I should call Lee she thought to herself. She looked at the clock. It was midnight. He'll be asleep. She sat on the bed holding the card. She hadn't talked to him since she left the hotel. It had been almost two weeks. "He'll just fuss," she said as she began to undress. She turned on the radio and lay on the bed, "okay, okay, okay," she said, as she began to dial his number.

"Lee, you sleep."

"Ma-Me, thank God—"

"I'm fine Lee."

"Ma-Me, you need to come home."

"No, I knew I shouldn't have called you."

"Ma-Me don't hang up. It's Nanmu she had a heart attack.

I Blew God a Kiss

Lee went to the Porter house the next day to see Joseph. When he pulled up in his shinny black Corvette, all the kids in the yard stopped in their tracks. He eased out of the car draped in silk. He handed the biggest boy in the yard a dollar to keep an eye on his car. All the kids started screaming at him for money. He reached in his pocket and pulled out a hand full of change. He handed out quarters until he ran out. He smelled barbecue coming from the back but decided to go through the front. He didn't want his clothes smelling of smoke.

Lee was the only son of doctors, Collin and Anita Sims. His parents met in medical school and they married shortly after Collin set up his medical practice.

He had known the Porter's all his life. His mom had delivered all the Porter children and his dad was their family doctor.

His father went ballistic when Lee decided to pursue a career in journalism instead of the medical field. His two older sisters had already followed in their parents footsteps. His oldest sister was a nurse and the other was a medical resident. Yet his father conceded when he realized how passionate his son was about his work as a critic and record promoter.

When Sadie saw Lee she went berserk. She started shouting hysterically at him.

"You took my baby from me," she kept repeating. Lizzie held her back and tried to calm her down.

"Sadie this Lee. You drunk. Ma-Me ain't with him."

"Ain't drunk. Get your hands off me! He sent my baby to New York. You ain't welcome in my house. Get out!" She yelled.

Joseph came in from the kitchen and escorted Lee out the front door.

Lee was trembling.

"You okay man," Joseph said when he got him outside.

"I don't know man," he said shaking his head.

"Sadie's bark is worst than her bite. Her world is falling apart. She has to have somebody to fight. I am sorry it had to be you."

"Thanks for rescuing me," he said as he was shaking Joseph's hand.

"Sure, man."

"How is Nanmu?"

"Holding her own. Nanmu is a strong woman."

"I came because I received a call from Ma-Me last night."

"Thank God!"

"That's what I said."

"How is she?"

"Stubborn as ever. I tried to talk her into coming home. She said she would call me back tonight."

"I am going to New York. I talked to Jay Pee and he thinks I should come and get Ma-Me."

I Blew God a Kiss

"I don't think she'll come back, not to stay anyway. She's concerned about Nanmu, but I don't know if that will get her back."

"I know I hurt her and I need to try to make it right somehow."

"Joe, Mrs. Sadie is right; if it wasn't for me, Ma-Me wouldn't had the money to leave here. I would give anything to take that back."

"It's not your fault man. She would have sought Vicky eventually."

"Ma-Me called me collect. This is the number she called me from," Lee said handing him a piece of paper. He hugged him and said, "Let me know if there is anything I can do to help."

After finding out about Nanmu, Layla worked hard at the store to keep from getting depressed. She was still angry but she wanted desperately to rush home to see Nanmu. She liked working in the store. There were all kinds of people coming in and out. She especially liked Pebbles a beautiful transvestite. Pebbles wasn't like most of the cross-dressers that Layla had been in contact with since she arrived in New York. Mr. Kerr had to tell her that he was a man. She would have never known. He had an elegant fashion sense. He had perfectly shaped waist and full hips. Layla wondered how his breast could be larger than hers. His makeup and nails looked as if he had a personal makeup artist and nail tech living at his house. He didn't overemphasize his feminine side; he was naturally ladylike. His voice wasn't harsh or rough. He spoke softly and calmly.

"Hi Miss Pebbles," Layla said when he entered the store.

"Hey, Miss Layla," Pebbles smiled and walked over to the

pop cooler.

A slender black guy came up to the register with a six-pack and asked Layla for a pack of Kools. Layla had seen him in the store several times. Mr. Kerr told her he was bad news so she didn't say much to him. He asked her name.

"You don't sound like you from New York. Where you from?"

"Alabama," she replied.

"A Bama, kid. I knew that was a southern accent. I got's people down there. Where 'bouts you from?"

"Grassy Creek."

"Really, is that any where near Paw Creek?"

"No, I never heard of that," she looked a little puzzled.

He started laughing. "I'm jiving, there ain't no Paw Creek. You have a nickname Layla. You know people in the south don't use their real names. I thank they be running from the Feds or something. They got names like Cricket, Cat, Squirrel, Gator, Butter, and my favorite Tree Head. How do you get a nickname like Tree Head?"

Layla was laughing so hard that tears started running down her face because what he was saying was true.

She was so busy with the other customers; Layla didn't notice Reggie walking in. Reggie looked like a rock star. He had blond stringy hair and bangs that covered his eyes. His lips were thin, almost invisible. He wore his shirt unbuttoned to his navel. Layla didn't understand why he wanted to show off his chest. It was smooth like a baby's bottom and no muscles. She wondered how he found her since she hadn't given him her address.

"Well if it isn't *Just Layla,*" he said smiling as he approached the register.

Layla didn't respond. It bothered her that he was there.

"You don't dance with a guy and just run out on him," he said this time with no smile.

"I am working," she said.

"What time you off—Just Layla?"

"Why?"

"I would like to take you to dinner."

"I am busy and if you don't want to buy anything I need to get back to work."

"Oh it's like that."

"Yeah, it's like that."

He turned and walked toward the door. He spun around and tossed his hair out of his eyes. He gave her a wicked look and pointed his index finger at her.

Layla couldn't sleep that night. She kept having nightmares about Reggie. She called Nia and asked if she had given him her address. Nia said that he probably followed them home after the party. She had heard some horrifying stories about him and thought he was doing time for child molestation. Nia told her to watch her back and if he came back around to call the police. That bit of news did not help Layla sleep any better.

When Layla awoke the next morning she called Jordan. She needed to be comforted and she was worried about Nanmu. Jordan cried when he heard her voice. He wanted to reach into the phone and grab her and he told her so.

"Jay Pee we have a lot to talk about," tears were flowing as she spoke.

"Ma-Me I am so sorry that we hurt you. You know how much I love you," he said.

"I know, I know," she whispered softy.

"Ma-Me, Nanmu is in intensive care. I am planning to leave this afternoon. I want you to come with me. I can book you on the flight with me. Ma-Me will you come?"

"Yes Jay Pee, I'll come."

"Good, I'll come and get you."

"No Jay Pee, I need to take care of some things here. What time does the plane leave? I can meet you at the airport."

"Ma-Me are you sure?"

"Jay Pee you know I've never lied to you. I'll be there."

"Meet me at the United ticket counter at 2 o'clock."

Layla knew that if she went home that it wasn't going to be easy making it back to New York. She was counting on her friendship with Mr. Kerr. She couldn't tell him how long she would be gone. He understood and was happy to know she was going to be with family. "Family is everything," he said.

Layla walked out of Mr. Kerr's looking forward to seeing her brother. She thought about Mr. Kerr's words; they reminded her of the many sermons that Nanmu had given her about staying connected to the family at all cost. She needed to stop at La Dea's. She knew her family would try to keep her in Alabama so she needed to secure her place at the school. She wanted to have something to come back for.

As she was hailing a cab Reggie came up behind her and pressed a gun in her back.

"You scream and I will kill you right here," he said. She took

I Blew God a Kiss

a deep breath and he said again, "I swear I'll drop you right here," he walked her into the alley where he parked his car. "Get in and put these on," he threw some handcuffs in her lap, "I want to hear them click."

When he got in the car he pulled her by her hair hard. "You think you better than me or something? You are going to regret the day you were born," she pulled away from him and he slapped her on the back of her head.

Through her tears she mumbled, "What do you want with me?"

"I want you to bleed. Then I want you to praise Reggie for making it stop."

I Blew God a Kiss

Jordan waited until 2:30 for Layla but she didn't show. He felt that something terrible was wrong. Layla had given her word. He talked with Mr. Kerr and he relayed to him that she had left for the airport over an hour before. Jordan's anxiety was running high; he didn't know what to think. He waited another 30 minutes then he put a hold on the tickets. He called Frankie and asked if could meet him at the office.

Frankie had disobeyed Jordan and continued to watch Layla, but he wasn't around her when he found out she was going home with Jordan. He knew that she was spending time with Nia. When he met with Jordan he brought all the information he had on Nia. Jordan asked Frankie if he would call Nia. He felt that she wouldn't be receptive to a black man calling asking questions about Layla.

"Nia Sun, you don't know me but I am a friend of Layla Porter. She was scheduled to fly to Alabama today, but she didn't make it to the airport. I was wondering— have you heard from her?" Frankie asked.

"She called, said she on her way to airport," she said sounding startled.

"Nia, what time was that?"

"About noon."

"Do you know if she was going anywhere else?"

"She said she go to La Dea modeling agency. To drop off photos."

"Nia, this is very important. Did Layla have a boyfriend that maybe she needed to say good-bye to?"

"Oh, my God!"

"Nia what is it? Please," Frankie pleaded.

"This guy follow her home form party. She said he show up in store yesterday. He jagged cause Layla blew him off. He bad news. He kidnapped my friend. She been in and out hospital every since."

"What's his name?"

"Reggie, Reggie Wallace."

"Do you know where he lives?"

"No, he's in and out of jail. I call some people. See if anybody know where we find him."

"Thanks Nia, we'll stay in touch."

Frankie gave Nia all his numbers including his pager. He asked her to call him if she heard anything.

Frankie talked with Jordan about everything that Nia had said and suggested that they call the police. Jordan said the police wouldn't do anything for twenty-four hours.

"Do we need to call Vicky?" Frankie asked.

"Yes, I'll call. I need you to run a check on this, this... fellow," he said, snapping his fingers.

"Reggie, you bet," Frankie said.

I Blew God a Kiss

"If he hurts my sister there won't be a hole deep enough for him to crawl in," Jordan said with rage.

"Don't you worry man, we'll find her," Frankie said.

"You know, I almost went to jail for something I didn't do. I spent almost a week locked up."

Frankie sat down on the sofa in Jordan's office.

"No kidding," he said.

"Yeah, I worked for this redneck who hated blacks, especially educated blacks. Do you know he didn't like me because of the way I talked? Can you believe that?"

"Yeah man, I can believe it."

"I left the job because my folks had a fight. I went looking for my old man. Someone robbed the A&P. They shot one of the cashiers. My boss Mr. Scotty told the police that I was one of the guys who did it. Knowing it wasn't me. The cops took his word over mine. They arrested me and did not set a bail. Nummu sent for Vicky to represent me. I was out within 24 hours after she got there. That was the worst time of my life. You know I wanted to kill myself in there. I was called mama's boy by kids I went to school with. After a few days of being threatened by some of the prisoners I wanted to kill myself. I received a picture from Ma-Me everyday. One day I was real low and my old man brought me a picture that she had drawn for me. It was of two men picking berries, it read. You need to finish this story. I always read her stories before she went to sleep. One night I started telling her this story about two men picking blackberries. She fell asleep before I could finish the story. When I saw that picture it gave me a reason to live. It was Vicky who came and rescued me from that lying Mr. Scotty, but it was Ma-Me who saved my life," he was silent a moment.

"I can't lose her, Gotti, I can't lose her," Jordan continued, "I knew where she was. I should have gone to get her. I know she listens to me. What was I thinking?"

"How did Vicky clear you? Frankie asked with curiosity.

"Huh?" Jordan had the look of a deer in the headlights.

"Vicky, how did she get you out so quick?" Frankie waited for an answer.

Jordan stood up and looked around the room as if he was searching for something.

Then he said, "Let's take a walk."

Victoria's office was located on the corner of Broadway and Ann Street minutes away from City Hall. Jordan needed courage to talk about the events of his youth—that he had so cautiously tucked away in his consciousness. Jordan enjoyed lunch at Champs, a deli that was four blocks from the office. Their conversation on the way to the deli was about how they could find Layla. Frankie didn't press Jordan on his personal story.

When they arrived at Champs Jordan requested to be seated by the window. He ordered a honey glazed maple turkey sandwich and Frankie ordered a Genoa salami sandwich. When the waitress brought them their meal, Jordan was finally ready to talk. He asked for a refill on his tea and Frankie did the same.

"Gotti today is the first time that I have mentioned the events of my imprisonment since it happened. Vicky had me released into her custody as soon as she arrived in town. The media had already convicted me. I became a prisoner in my own home because of the verbal slander I received when I went out. My house was trashed and marked with all kind of racial slurs. Someone even tried to set the house on fire. Pop managed to put the flames out before they engulfed the porch."

"I am sorry to bring back painful memories, especially now. If you don't want to talk about it you don't have to," Frankie interjected.

"I want to. To be honest I have wanted to talk about it for a long time. My mom told me to forget that it happened. She felt that holding on to something that painful would stunt my growth. When I first came to this city, I was terrified. I could not walk down the street without having an anxiety attack. One day I started walking and found this place. It is now one of my favorite spots," he said looking around the deli.

"I like it to," Frankie said.

"It wasn't a difficult task for Vicky to clear me. The prosecution botched the investigation. They had a witness that swore I was not one of the perpetrators. The girl that was shot, she knew all those dudes. Her boyfriend was the one who shot her. He found out that she was messing around. The police had not bothered to question her. I never went to trial. Vicky threaten to sue the whole lot of them; so the judge dropped the case. Vicky knows the right questions to ask."

"What happened to Mr. Scotty?"

"Man, Vicky brought him up on charges for obstructing justice. Mr. Scotty was astute—I heard he was acquitted. He admitted that he made a mistake. He said he thought one of them looked like me. I hate my family was put through that ordeal. Now, let's go and find my sister. My moms can't handle too many more tragedies."

Frankie Petro was not his real name. His name was Francesco Grosso of the Grosso crime family of Littly Italy in the Bronx. He changed his name to Petro after the historical Joseph Petrosino. Petrosino was famous for eradicating crime from Little Italy in the 1900's. He was known as the Sherlock Holmes of Little Italy. Frankie loved hearing the stories told about him and he especially liked that his dad hated hearing his name. Jordan gave Frankie the nickname of Gotti. It was the name of an Italian friend he knew from college.

Frankie's mom tried to do all she could to keep him out of the syndicate. She died his last semester of college. When his mom died, he dropped out of school and started working for Victoria. After the funeral, he severed all contact with his father. Five years had past since they spoke.

Frankie had a loathsome feeling that Layla wasn't alive. He thought about how innocent she looked when he first saw her. He knew his dad had the resources to find Reggie. He didn't want to use his dad's muscle.

He decided to call his friend Sergeant Miles at police headquarters to see if he could get a recent address on Reggie. Miles gave him the address for Rebecca Masters who lived-in Tribeca. She owned a small art gallery and stayed in a back room.

When he entered Master's gloomy room it smelled of old socks. The art displayed on the walls and tables looked as if a blind man had painted them. They had no form or structure. The images were as if they had taken all the primary colors and thrown them together to make a weird dreadful looking shade of color. You would

I Blew God a Kiss

have to be stoned to buy this stuff, he thought. When he saw Rebecca, he understood. She was a spindly looking redhead. She had round bright eyes that were fixed in a sunken face. She had obviously seen a lot of hard years.

Frankie introduced himself and asked if she was the artist of this incredible art.

"You like it?" She asked, with a half grin on her face.

"It's incredible," he said.

"This be a nice piece for your bedroom," she said picking up a bizarre looking painting from one of the tables.

"Yes it would," he said, "but I am here for some information."

"You's a cop?" She looked at him with gazing eyes.

"No, I am looking for a friend of mine. I have reason to believe that she is with Reggie Wallace."

She turned and walked away, "I can care less about that pig. He owes me three grand."

"Maybe you help me find him I get your bread," Frankie said.

"Hah, you and what army? Reggie cares nothing about nobody, not even himself. You can't scare him. I fear for your friend. I can't help you. He knows where I live."

"She has a family that will pay a reward to get her back."

"How much reward?" She asked a little more interested.

"Let's just say her mom has deep pockets."

"If you find him based on the information I give, you'll take care of me."

"Guaranteed!" He said, as he extended his hand out to shake

hers.

"There's a couple of places he goes when he don't want to be found. I suggest you don't go alone." She started handing him a piece of paper and then snatched it back when he reached for it. "You's gots to do something for me, now," she said.

He reached in his pocket and pulled out two fifties and gave them to her.

"Don't worry, if I find her you'll be taken care of."

Jordan entered the train station as if he were in a daze. He watched as the people interacted with one another but he was not hearing any sounds. His body was present in the station but his mind was far removed. He didn't notice Joseph when he walked up to him.

"Son, Son," Joseph said shaking his arms.

When Jordan saw Joseph, he didn't feel the hatred that had sustained him for so many years. Layla had been missing for two days. The police had not given them much hope of her whereabouts. Jordan was functioning on little sleep and it was apparent in the depth of his eyes. Joseph hugged Jordan for a long time without saying a word. They walked out of the train station and Victoria was waiting for them in her car. She stepped out to greet him. She reached out her hand to give Joseph a handshake. Jordan opened the car door and sat in the backseat.

"Ah, suky, suky, now—come here woman," Joseph said as he took hold of her hand and pulled her close to him.

"Same old Joe Joe," she said smiling, "Get in the car!"

They rode alone silent for awhile. The sounds of the New

I Blew God a Kiss

York traffic were like a symphony, every part played its own distinct sound. Finally Joseph broke the silence.

"So, Frankie know where Ma-Me is," he said tapping his fingers on the dash.

"Yes sir," Jordan piped in as if rising from the dead.

"Joseph," Victoria began, "we wanted you to come because Frank believes that this Reggie character might have sold Ma-Me."

"Sold—what do you mean sold?" Joseph asked outraged.

"Pop—" Jordan's voice trembled.

"Joe we are hoping that it's not true but she wasn't with Reggie when Frankie found him and well maybe we need to let Frank tell you what he got out of him."

"Where is Frankie now?" Joseph asked.

"He's waiting for us at Jordan's apartment."

"And this Reggie fellow where is he?"

"You don't want to know," Jordan said with fire in his eyes.

They pulled up to Jordan's apartment building. The world around them seemed normal. There was a guy on the corner selling hotdogs and pretzels. The children were jumping double-dutch, hopscotch, riding their bikes and playing jacks. There was a group of girls singing, clapping and dancing in front of the door. Joseph stopped to watch them. Jordan continued to the door. He had seen them there a hundred times. To him they no longer existed. The rhythmic sounds reminded Joseph of the military cadence. One kid would sing and the other kids would respond with the word check.

"My name is Dawn."

"Check."

"I live in Queens."

"Check."

"I am-the meanest—girl on the scene."

They all would laugh and then retort, "Check".

C ome on dear; let's get you a nice hot bath." A gentle voice whispered to her.

She knew the voice didn't belong to Reggie. Her vision couldn't recognize the figure that was helping her.

"You'll feel better once you've eaten."

She tried to say something but the words would not form. He led her down a long corridor. The hall consisted of about ten doors. He took her in one of the rooms and laid her on the bed.

"Lay here I am going to run you a bath. Don't worry. I won't hurt you."

She wondered what had happened to Reggie. The last thing she remembered he was beating her for spitting in his face. Could this guy have come along and helped her? She tried to adjust her eyes so she could see who he was. Why can't I see? She thought.

"Your bath is ready," he said gently, "let me help you."

She noticed flickers of lights surrounding the tub. The aroma of almonds, honey and vanilla started to revive her. The water felt soothing to her aching skin. Her head fell on a pillow as she sank into the tub.

I Blew God a Kiss

"That's it. You just lay there and relax. I'll get you some fruit and something to drink. I'll be back."

Layla didn't know how long she had lain in the tub. The water had cooled down and her vision had returned. She looked around the room. There were mirrors covering every wall. The tub was the room's single object; it expanded six foot by six foot around the room. The pillow followed the tub's circumference.

Layla had never seen anything like it. As she started to get out of the tub, she noticed there were no doors. As she contemplated how to get out of the mirrored room, one of the mirrored panels opened. It frightened her, and she scrambled to get out of the tub.

"Woe woe woe, sweet pea. Calm down. We don't want you to drown."

Layla recognized the voice and calmed down.

"Who are you and what am I doing here?"

"I'm Tootie. I'm here to take care of you," he said holding out a big towel for her to step into.

"What is this place?" She reached for the towel and covered herself.

"I have some food for you. Come I have the table set," he said avoiding her question.

She followed Tootie into a lilac colored room. Everything was lilac including the bed; it had a lilac fur cover a little darker than the fur rugs on the floor. The room had a small dining area that sat just inside a set of French doors which led to a balcony. The table was enticing, with a full spread of fresh fruits, vegetables and roast duck. Tootie guided Layla to a chair. He served them both small portions then began to talk nonstop as if he had known her all his life. Layla stared at the constant movement of his mouth but didn't comprehend what he was talking about.

"What you mean, you're my partner?"

"I want jive you. You seem like a cherry so I'll give it to you straight. We make movies here, porn movies you dig."

Layla nodded.

He continued, "There are ten of us. We each have a partner. I've been here for nine months. I ended up here by that chop who brought you here. I thought he was cool. I was hitch hiking from Boston when he picked me up. My old man didn't dig me. He called me a punk sissy and tried to beat the faggot out of me. That's funny, how do you beat something out that's not there? So I left home. I've been told that I'm a little feminine. I will admit that I used it sometimes to survive. My last partner in here was a man. His name was Peter. The sweetest person I have ever known," he was silent for a moment sitting there shaking his head. Then he started talking again. This time he did not talk as fast. His words were slow and dragging.

"He hated it here. He was from Chicago. He was in New York on vacation. He stepped in a joint his last night in the city and someone slipped him a Mickey. The next day I was bathing and feeding him. He tried to escape three times. The third time they made an example of him," Tootie stopped talking.

His words caused Layla to panic. She began crying hysterically. "I can... can't stay here... hee," she cried.

Tootie walked over and put his arms around her, "I know, I know."

When Joseph entered the apartment Victoria was coming out

of the bathroom, Jordan, Frankie and two Italian men where in the living room. Frankie introduced them as Marco and Luciano. Marco said. "Buon giorno." Luciano just nodded. They both sat around Jordan's bar while Joseph and Victoria sat on the sofa. Jordan and Frankie stood up.

"Mr. Porter your daughter is in New Jersey," Frankie said.

"How sure are you?" Joseph asked.

"I'm a hundred percent sure. Reggie would not have lied not after we worked him over."

Luciano hit his fist in his hand.

Frankie paused for a minute and then he continued, "We can go in and get her, but I don't know if it would be clean. There are at least three bodyguards on duty at all times. The place is not easy to penetrate. The weak spot is they send their laundry out twice a day, 8am and again at 8pm."

"What about some police help?" Victoria responded.

"I talked to Sergeant Miles. They don't have any jurisdiction in Jersey, and he can't involve the Jersey PD without proof," Frankie answered.

"What about Reggie? He took her there, couldn't he be a witness?" Joseph asked.

"Mr. Porter, I am sorry but Reggie won't be useful. No! We are on our own. We can do it," he said looking at his buddies that were seated on the bar stools.

"You're not leaving me out of this," Jordan piped in.

"Me either, I've never backed down from a fight a day in my life. Let's do this," Joseph added.

"Mrs. Vicky, I think you need to go in the other room. When

this goes down I don't want you to be involved."

"I'm not a putts Frankie. I don't need your protection. I am staying," she rebuked him.

"Alright then let's get started.

Compelled by a force he did not understand Frankie was a man driven. He wanted Layla out of that nightmare. Was it because of her youthful innocence or beauty? He did not know. All he knew was something had latched itself onto him and wouldn't let loose. What a strange and leery feeling it was. The irony was the violence he hated his dad for had now become a part of his life. His father's words played repeatedly in his head.

"You spit on your grandfather's name," his dad said, "and now you come to me for help."

When he turned to walk away his father pulled him back and said, "You remind me of your madre. I give you what you need."

Five years of anger and hate stood between them, yet Layla's need had become their fulfillment. His father gave him Marco and Luciano. Frankie had his regrets after Reggie met his untimely demise. He hardened his heart and justified the murder, blaming it on Reggie's own arrogance and stupidity. Reggie asked Marco what did a bunch of greasers want with a nigger woman. That infuriated Luciano and he lost control. He beat him continuously in the head with his pistol.

Frankie had blueprints of the estate where they held Layla captive. He sat on the floor and placed them on Jordan's glass coffee table.

"The name of the cleaning service is Nellie's. We'll need the driver, otherwise we will draw suspicion. We have two choices. We can pay off the driver or we can take him by force," Frankie said.

"We will pay him," Victoria said.

"Are you sure?" Joseph questioned.

"How much can a laundry driver make? Yea, quite sure," she answered.

They planned throughout the evening. Frankie suggested that everyone go home and get some rest. They would go in during the evening pick-up. It would give them a chance to locate the driver.

The estate was secluded in a rural area. It was not visible from any street. Up close however it was a magnificent place. A red oak sat by the lake. Its limbs were lowered to the ground like an octopus reaching for a drink of water. The road that led to the estate ran along side of the lake; the house sat about a quarter mile back from the lake. It was a split-level Victorian home with a huge wrap around porch. There was an alley to the left and a sign that read; "Please deliver packages to the rear."

Frankie gave the driver five thousand dollars. That was all it took for him to turn over the use of his truck. The driver's helpfulness provided them with the easiest way to get into the house. He suggested they ultilize the laundry carts. He said they never checked them. Frankie and Marco went in. They overpowered the two men guarding the back entrance then motioned for the others to come in.

They were able to rescue Layla without incident from the hands of Gabriel Goldie better known as Gee Gee to the scum world of porn. The police arrested Goldie for kidnapping and murder. It trilled Tootie to testify and get justice for his friend Peter. An ambulance took Layla to a nearby hospital where she was treated for dehydration and a fractured rib.

As she lie in bed hooked up to monitors and an IV drip, her heroic rescuers visited her. First Jordan arrived; he lay in bed with her and put his arms around her.

"There were two men in the blackberry patch," he said.

"Oh Jay Pee," Layla cried.

"Hey this is a story I never got a chance to finish." He kissed her on the top of her head. "You see these two men in the berry patch almost had two full pails of blackberries when one of them spotted a bear."

"Jay Pee—a bear in the blackberry patch."

"Whose story is this anyway?"

"Okay, finish."

"Well the one who spotted him yelled, 'Bear!' And he took off running. The other dropped his pail and took off behind him. 'We are never going to outrun this bear,' one of them yelled at the other. 'You're right. I can't run anymore. Let's stop and pray.' As they got on their knees to pray the bear caught up with them. 'Hey wait a minute,' the bear said to them. 'You fellows are Christians.' 'Yeah!' They both said at the same time looking at each another bewildered. 'Well how about that,' the bear said. 'What a small world this is. What are the chances? I am a Christian bear.' 'No kidding,' said one of the fellows. 'Wow what a relief,' said the other. 'Well, let's pray,' the bear said. So the bear knelt down between the two men. He put one hand on the shoulder of the one man and the other hand on his buddy's shoulder. Then he looked up toward heaven and he started to pray, 'Lord you have been good to me and I just want to thank you for all your goodness. You have brought me your servants, my fellow brothers and I thank you for that. And Lord I thank you for this my food I am about to receive."

"Oh, Jay Pee, you are awful," Layla laughed, "Jay Pee?"

"Yes, Ma-Me."

"I knew you would come."

"Ma-Me I am sorry I didn't tell you about Mrs. Vicky."

"It don't seem to be that important no more."

"Knock, knock, can we come in," Joseph said walking in with Victoria and Frank.

Victoria was carrying a huge bouquet of flowers. Frankie had a single rose. Jordan got out of the bed and sat in one of the chairs. Joseph leaned over and planted a smacker on Layla's lips and asked. "How is my best girl?" Layla hugged Joseph and kissed him on the neck.

"Sweetheart, I want you to meet someone," Joseph said to her, "This is Frank Petro, we would not have found you without him."

"Please to meet you Sunshine," Frankie said as he laid the rose beside her.

"Is it okay to give you a hug?" Layla asked him.

"You betcha," he said, they both had tears in their eyes as they embraced.

Jordan motioned to Frankie and they both left the room. Joseph reached out for Victoria's hand.

"Ma-Me, this is not how I imagined this moment. This is… well, I will leave you two alone so you can get to know each other," he left the room.

Victoria married William Gentry a millionaire like her father who owned cotton mills and real estate in four states. She did not love him but money marries money. It's just the way it was done. He was old enough to be her father so there wasn't much intimacy. She bore him a son. He wanted someone to leave his legacy to. She named him Michael Carter. Carter was her mother's maiden name. As she sat there gazing on her lovely adult daughter, her fortune did not matter. She longed for forgiveness knowing, that she did not deserve it for what she had done seventeen years ago. It was a foolish rebellious act that grew out of her curiosity of wanting to have sex with a black man. Victoria never told her family of Layla's existence because she knew the consequences would not be pleasant. Her father had her whole life mapped out for her, and she did not want to disappoint him. That's not the real reason she gave Layla to Joseph. There were plenty of excuses she had come up with over the years many of them helped her to sleep soundly. Sitting there at that moment she knew why. She did not want a black child. She never considered herself to be prejudice; she was a civil rights activist and one of the largest contributors to the NAACP.

"Layla, I don't know how to say forgive me for giving you away. I thought it was the right decision at the time," she said after a long silence.

"What about five years later or ten? What about fifteen," Layla said angrily.

"I deserve that. It wasn't that easy. Joseph or Sadie would not have—"

"Would not have what? Let you come back and get your black daughter. Do you know how hard it has been for me? Being too black too be white and to white to be black. I have hated you and my dad every since I found out. Both of you are selfish and I have paid my whole life for your selfishness. I can't accept you and I can't forgive either of you. I want to go home. I want to see Nanmu."

Layla's words were cutting and sharp to Victoria heart. She was a hard woman and did not allow Layla to see the pain she caused her. She stood up and said. "I will let your father know." She kissed Layla on the forehead and walked out of the room.

Victoria went to Joseph and told him that Layla was ready to go home. He didn't question her. He lightly touched her arm and nodded. Then he went to Layla's room. Jordan knew Victoria and he could tell the meeting with Layla did not go well.

"I need a cigarette," she said to him.

"Vicky you don't smoke," Jordan replied.

"I do today," she said.

An orderly was walking by and she asked him where they could find the cafeteria. He pointed them to the elevator and said to take the second floor and turn right when you get off.

Jordan followed her remaining silent as they walked. She found a cigarette machine in a small room off the main floor of the cafeteria. She fumbled through her purse looking for change. Jordan reached in his pocket and pulled out a hand full of quarters. She selected a pack of Virginia Slims.

"I need a light Jordan," she said flipping the cigarette at him.

"I'll be right back," he said.

He returned a couple minutes later with a lighter. She leaned against the wall and took a slow deep draw. She held it in for a long time. She took another draw and repeated this procedure a few more times. Finally she spoke.

"I smoked once. I quit when I got pregnant with Layla. This is the first cigarette I've had since the day I found out that I was pregnant. I thought I made the right chose giving her to your dad. It sure as hell was the right one for me," she cut her eyes over at Jordan. The remark she made did not please him.

"Don't look at me like that Jordan. You have no idea what it was like in my family."

"Oh, well tell me. Did your mama drink to drown her sorrow and did your dad leave home to be with some nineteen year old every chance he got? Did your parents fight every time your dad stepped through the door? Don't tell me about having it rough. You don't know what that means."

"That's not fair Jordan. What kind of life would Layla have if my father disinherited me?"

"Vicky you don't get it—do you?"

"What do you mean?"

"You are one of New York's top attorneys. Your old man didn't have anything to do with that. You are wealthy without him or that millionaire husband of yours. You didn't want Ma-Me because she was black."

"That's not true. How can you say that to me? You, of all people."

"Me, of all people, being the only black attorney in your firm. Is that what you mean?"

"No, that's not what I'm saying and you know it."

"I know if you want to make it right with Ma-Me, you need to start being honest with yourself about what you did," Jordan walked away from her enraged and annoyed. He reasoned that she

I Blew God a Kiss

would never understand.

I Blew God a Kiss

When Jordan returned to Layla's room, his father was standing outside. A doctor and two nurses were in the room.

"What happened?" Jordan assumed that his father had upset Layla and his anger showed on his tightly wrinkled face.

"She was having chills so I called the nurse. She has a fever of 103," Joseph said anguished.

Frankie, Marco and Luciano were sitting in a waiting room that was near the elevator. Jordan asked Frankie if he would ask Victoria to come to Layla's room right away. When Frankie returned with Victoria the doctor was coming from the room.

"She is going to be fine. I gave her something for the fever and I am prescribing an antibiotic. I am drawing some blood. I believe she has an infection," the doctor said.

"What sort of infection?" Victoria asked.

"I won't know until I get the results from the test," he answered, "I gave her something to help her rest," he continued, "I suggest you do the same. She'll be fine."

Frankie gave Victoria a hug. "I booked rooms at the Hyatt.

It's about a half hour from here," he said.

"No, I don't want to leave," she said.

"Vicky, you and Pop get some rest. I'll stay with her. If there are any changes I'll call you," Jordan said.

"No, I want to stay Jordan. You go with your dad, please," she begged.

"Come on son, Frankie," Joseph said, he nodded at Marco and Luciano.

Frankie finally being at peace with Layla's safety joined his comrades Marco and Luciano and headed back to New York. With sincerity and gratefulness, Jordan gave Frankie a high five.

Joseph needed to call Sadie to give her the news of their daughter. Jordan suggested he waited until they checked into the hotel.

Layla remained in the hospital a few days. Then the three of them headed back to Alabama. The communication on the journey home was to a minimum. Having Layla safe was a comfort to both Joseph and Jordan and they each were secure in their silence.

Sadie summoned the family that Layla was returning so the usual Porter-Bailey reunion was set. However Layla could not bare the crowd and asked to be taken to the hospital to be with Nanmu who was out of intensive care.

Nanmu lost a considerable amount of weight but she was still vibrant and strong. She seemed more confident in her faith.

"Come here child," she said to Layla when she entered the room. "Praise be, the Lord has answered my prayers. You are a sight for sore eyes," she hugged her and held on to her as if she would never let her go.

I Blew God a Kiss

"Look in that drawer over there and get me my brush," Nanmu said.

Lalya took the brush from the drawer and proceeded to brush Nanmu's hair.

"Ma-Me I want to brush your hair," she said.

Layla continued to brush her hair as if she did not hear her. Tears began to stream down her face as she brushed.

"I knew Jay Pee would find you. He has an instinct about him, that boy, when it comes to you. Remember that day when the judge dropped those charges they had on him and we went to the river to celebrate?"

"Yes'em," Layla said.

She laughed that laugh that comes deep from the soul that only Nanmu possess.

"You wandered off like you often do to explore in the woods. I told Jay Pee to go find you. He said he found you sitting in a tree. Why were you in that tree child?"

Layla stopped brushing Nanmu's hair and sat on the bed beside her.

"I knew Jay Pee would come. I climbed the tree to wait for him."

"Were you ever afraid?"

"No mam. I saw a butterfly and started chasing it. That's how I got off the path. Jay Pee always said that if I ever got lost in the woods to wait for him, he would find me."

"He is a fine boy," Nanmu said proudly.

"Nanmu, bad things happened to me. All my life I have been teased for being with a black family. I thought that if people thought

I was white, they would treat me differently. And for a while I was. Then something very dark happened," Layla froze a wave of fear brushed against her.

Nanmu felt it too and said loudly," I rebuke you devil—leave this room in Jesus name!"

Layla gave Nanmu a hug.

"Go on child, don't be afraid," Nanmu said.

"Nanmu, I thought I was going to die. He kept telling me that he had a grave with my name on it and when he finished with me, he was going to put me in it. I thought he was just trying to scare me. Then he took me to this cemetery. There it was a grave freshly dug. I never was so scared in all my life," tears flowed down her cheeks, "I knew I was going to die," she repeated.

Nanmu interrupted her, "fetch me that pitcher of water and those two cups."

Layla obeyed and Nanmu poured them both a cup of water. Nanmu waited until Layla was calm enough to talk again.

"He pushed me down at the edge of the grave and was saying foul and nasty words to me. All the while saying he was going to bury me. Then I wasn't afraid any more. I thought about you. I remember when you would blow kisses to me when I was little when I didn't want you to leave me. You would tell me that your kisses would keep you close to me. Right then and there—I blew God a kiss. The next thing I knew I was in this place being taken care of by the most sensitive man. Reggie drugged me and sold me to this place that make naked movies. I know that God took me out of his hands and I knew he would send Jay Pee to rescue me."

"You are a special child Layla Renee Porter. Just keep your

I Blew God a Kiss

hands in the Lord's hand and everything will be alright."

Through clenched teeth and painful sobs, Layla held on to Nanmu, she said, "He did some things to me that I just can't say."

Layla's eyes showed an anger and hatred that Nanmu had never seen in her before. Nanmu said a silent prayer, "Lord please save my granddaughter."

Nanmu remained in the hospital for several more days. Layla was not ready to return home and she asked Nanmu if she could stay with her. Sadie did not like the idea. She couldn't comprehend Layla's resolve not to come home. Despite all that had happened, Sadie still refused to give up her claim as Layla's biological mother. Joseph wanted to get her some professional help, but that only led to more fights.

Nanmu's home was like a revolving door of people coming in and out from sun up until midnight and some even stayed overnight. It was Lizzie, Juanita and Sam who were there most often. They cooked, cleaned, shopped did laundry and even bathed Nanmu. Nanmu was a proud woman but she craved the attention and radiated like the sun.

Layla didn't mind all the people, but sometimes she had to get away from Lizzie's husband Roy with his obnoxious jokes and attitude. They had two sons, Ricky and Calvin. Calvin was quiet and kept to himself but Ricky was sociable and fun loving. He would take Layla with him whenever they felt squeezed in by all the people. He had a 1966 Plymouth Valiant, cream colored with red interior. His front license plate read; Big Eagle. He worshiped that car, and there wasn't a speck on it.

Layla was vulnerable. Her childhood innocence had been

swept away. She felt relaxed and comfortable around Ricky. He made her laugh and that felt good to her.

"You know Ma-Me, since Aunt Sadie's not your real mama that mean, you ain't my cousin."

"Don't even think about it Ricky. You still family," she stood her ground even after a hundred advances.

He turned on his eight track tape recorder that was playing The Temptations. He handed her a joint and told her to fire it up. She lit the joint and took a couple of hits and then handed it to him.

"How is your side? Are you still hurting? There is a party cross-town you want to go?" He asked as he held in the smoke.

"I'm not ready for no party."

"You can't stay locked up in that shell of yours Ma-Me. What happened to you in New York?"

"Nothing, can you stop and get us something to drink?"

"Yeah, you want some beer or some wine?"

"Beer."

He pulled over at a corner store and returned with a six-pack. As he handed her a beer he said to her, "I won't let anything happen to you."

They drove around for awhile singing and laughing until the beer and marijuana was gone. Then they went back to Nanmu's and sat in the car watching as their family members sneaked around the house to drink their booze.

That same night Jordan was taking care of Sadie he did not realize that her mind was slipping. He was confident that he could nurse her back or convince her to seek help. He had to earn her trust because she believed that everyone was against her. He desperately tried to force her to eat. She was in bed for two days and had not eaten. He spent the day shopping and cleaning so he was weary and his patience with her was running thin.

"Jay Pee, you my good boy," she said pushing the bowl of soup away from her.

"Mama please eat just a few bites. It's your favorite chicken noodle."

"Jay Pee, I want you to bring my baby home, she left me Jaay Peee," her speech began to slur.

"Okay, mama, now eat."

"They say she not my baby. You know she my baby. You was there when she was born. Want you Jay Pee?"

"Yes, Mam, I was there."

"You tell 'em she is my child. You tell 'em, you hear."

"I'll tell them mama."

She grabbed him by the shirt and pulled him close to her, "You bring my baby home to me."

"Mama, if you promise me you will eat. I will bring her home. You got to be strong for her."

"Yeah, I must be strong," she reached for the bowl.

After she finished eating, Jordan kissed her on the forehead and told her to get some rest. His brother David was on the sofa watching TV. It was nine o'clock and his sister Juanita was not home. He sat down on the sofa.

"Do you know where your sister is?"

He didn't say a word he just shrugged his shoulders.

"Does she have any friends she hangs out with?"

"She spend time with Cockrite."

"Cockrite Mackey."

"Yeah."

"I am going to Nanmu's to talk with Ma-Me. You'll be alright."

"He nodded not taking his eyes off the TV.

I'll see if I can find your sister. I'll send her home. He patted him on the leg.

When Jordan arrived at Nanmu's house Ricky was sitting on the front porch steps. It was a balmy night so the front door was open and the chatter and laughter could be heard from the inside.

"Big E," Jordan said to him.

"Jay, what's happening?" Ricky asked.

"Looking for Ma-Me. Seen her?"

"She inside, helping Nanmu to bed."

He walked up the stairs stepping around him. Ricky made no attempt to move. Sam was sitting in an easy chair and Calvin lay asleep on the sofa. Everyone else was in the kitchen. He went up to where Sam was sitting and balled up his fist and gave him some dap. He pulled up a straight chair and sat beside him.

"Good to see you Jay Pee," Sam said.

"You too Uncle Sammy."

"How is working in New York?"

"It's real fine," he said with a slight smile.

"How long you here for?"

"Two weeks."

"That's good the family need you. I wish you could stay longer. You looking for Ma-Me?"

"Yeah."

I Blew God a Kiss

"I think you should know she been hanging with Ricky. She's a little loaded."

Jordan started to get up and Sam pulled him back down.

"Hold on don't be too hasty."

"Why didn't you try to stop this? You know she don't need to be with him."

"She's been through so much. The only time she smiles is when he is around. Jay Pee you can't always be her savior. You got to let it go. You put too much on yourself. You have since Ma-Me was a baby."

Layla walked into the room. When she saw Jordan she yelled. "Jay Pee, when you get here! Nanmu was just asking 'bout you. You should go say goodnight," she said giving him a hug.

"I'll let her rest. It's late. I'll see her tomorrow. Can we talk?"

"Sure, what's wrong Jay Pee?"

Sam stood up and said, "I am calling it a night."

"Good night Uncle Sammy." Layla said.

Jordan just nodded.

When Sam left the house, Layla asked Jordan again what was wrong.

"Ma-Me, I need you to come home, Mama need you."

"No, I won't go. She is not my mother."

"Ma-Me she is the only mother you know."

"The only mother I know; she has never been a mother to me and you know that. She just need me there to cook and clean. I am never going back. I am sick of cleaning her vomit and washing her pissed filled clothes."

"Ma-Me this ain't you. Just calm down. You don't mean that."

"You left me here Jay Pee. You don't know what I went through. I didn't have any friends at school, nobody wanted to be around the white coon." She yelled and everyone in the kitchen became silent.

"Okay, Ma-Me," Jay Pee said as he walked out the front door.

Ricky was standing by the door and Jordan brushed passed him real hard.

"Watch what you doing!" Ricky declared.

"Get out of my face, man," Jordan said pushing him away.

Layla stepped out the door and grabbed Ricky by the arm, "Let him go," she whispered.

"You see what he did," Ricky said, "he thinks he is better than me or something."

"No, he don't," Layla said.

"He act like you his woman instead of his sister. With his nose stuck up in the air like he holier-than-thou. He push me again I'm gone bust his face," he said raising his voice and shaking his fist at the air.

Lizzie poked her head out the door and asked what the fuss was about.

"Nothing, mama, go back inside."

"Boy, you don't tell me what to do. You know Nanmu ain't well and you out here keeping up all this ruckus."

"I was just leaving. Ma-Me, you coming?"

"No I 'm going to bed," she turned and went inside and said

goodnight to her aunt Lizzie.

Jordan knew that Layla was flying high yet it was as if she was a total stranger to him. Everything in him wanted to take the next train back to New York. Why do you have to be born into a family? Why can't we be like the birds? Once they leave the nest, they don't have to return. Those thoughts raced through his mind.

"I'm Jay Pee. I have always been her favorite. What is she doing with that chump Ricky? Can't she see he's not worth a nickel," he heard himself say, "I have to get him away from her."

I Blew God a Kiss

It was 5am when Juanita came in. Jordan was waiting up for her. When he confronted her with her whereabouts, she shunned him. His anger was still ignited from the previous night so in an instant he poured all his frustrations on his young sister. The action between them was so heated that it woke Sadie. When she entered the room Jordan had his hand raised to slap his sister. He lowered it when he saw his mother.

"What is this about?" Sadie asked as she tied her robe around her.

"I wish he would go back to where he came from. He needs to stay out my business," Juanita said with puffed lips.

"What kind of business you got. You only 13," Jordan said.

"I will handle this Jay Pee. You go to bed," Sadie said.

"Do you know she is pregnant?" He shouted almost at the point of tears.

"I can't take this right now. I can't take this," Sadie said returning to her room.

"This is just great," Jordan said as he left the house.

Jordan sat in the car until the sun came up. He reminisced

about all the wonders he missed about Alabama. He was never able to see the sun rising above the trees the way he saw it right now. He remembered lying on the roof on warm muggy nights naming the stars and fantasizing about being an astronaut. He loved the sweet smell of the dogwood trees and biting into a fresh sun raised peach. He prayed for his family then he prayed for himself. He could not believe he was going to hit his sister. He closed his eyes and could hear her say. "I am grown. I am having my own chile," he desperately needed Nanmu, but he didn't want to upset her. His dad had moved in with a Geechee woman so he decided to go to him. With the resolve to see his dad he took his mom's advise and went back inside to bed.

Naomi LaPlumb was an undeniable change for Joseph. She was in her mid-fifties and extremely wealthy. Rumor was that she acquired her wealth from her youthful years of being a Madame in New Orleans. Age and hard living had stripped away her glamorous face, but it didn't steal her pride and dignity. She had a certain air about her that gave an impression that she had lived among royalty.

It was one in the afternoon when she opened the door for Jordan. She was draped in expensive silk lingerie and wearing high heel shoes. Jordan complimented her on her beauty and asked if he could see his dad. She gracefully led him into a well decorated sitting parlor.

"Jay Pee."

"Pop," Jordan stood up and gave him a hug.

"Is something wrong, son? You not leaving are you. I thought you was taking some time off."

It's not that," he said as he sat down.

I Blew God a Kiss

"Okay," Joseph sat down in a fancy French chair across from him.

"Oh, I don't know where to start. Well, I guess I need to just say it. You should go back home."

Joseph laughed.

"This is not funny. This is your family.

"Son I am not going home. Forget it."

"Nita is pregnant."

"What! Who?"

"Cockrite Mackey."

"That drug dealing Cockrite. I will kill that son—"

"Yeah, well that's not all mama needs taken care of. I can't stay here and I can't return to New York with her the way she is. Do you know she is really sick?"

"Son, my going home would make things worse. Yo mama don't want me near her. I can bring Davie and Nita here."

"She couldn't handle not having any of her children around. I fear to think what would happen if you did that."

"I'll talk to the family and see if we can get her in a hospital."

"A mental hospital?"

"What else can we do? I can't help her. She has to stop drinking."

"You can help her if you want to. We're not committing her. No way!"

"Jay Pee, she needs professional help. I am not a doctor. She will die if she doesn't get the help she needs. Do you want that?"

"No, I don't want that, but I don't want to see her committed either."

"Well I'll talk to the family and see what we can do."

"You'll take care of Nita and Davie?"

"Yeah, I'll take care of them."

"I am taking Ma-Me to New York with me."

"I don't think that's a good idea not after what she went through up there."

"She is getting stoned with Big Eagle."

"Ma-Me wouldn't do that."

"She is not Ma-Me anymore. I have never seen so much anger in her before."

"Do you think she will even go back?" Joseph asked.

"I don't know. I will have to try."

They said their good-byes and Joseph promised that he would take care of Sadie.

Joseph walked in the bedroom with Naomi. He didn't know how she would take having children around and he wasn't quite ready to spring the news on her. His first resolve was to Sadie.

"Mek you doh rarry so?" She asked with her thick Gullah accent.

"I am worried because my son laid a heavy trip on me."

"E sweet mout me."

"Yeah, he has his daddy's charm."

"In yah cad side down."

He obeyed her and sat on the bed beside her. He began to pour his heart out to her conveying all that Jordan had shared with him.

"E long eye," she said.

I Blew God a Kiss

"Yeah, I know he is asking a lot. But I can't sit back and watch my family fall apart."

"Tie yuh mout."

He kept talking even after she told him not to. "I need to go and see about Sadie."

"Tie yuh mout," she repeated.

I Blew God a Kiss

Lee sat in his apartment unable to focus on his work. Layla was home for over a week and had not called him. He called her several times with no-good results. Her family would say she wasn't in or not taking any calls. This puzzled him. He thought their friendship could withstand anything. He couldn't get settled until he saw her.

Lee arrived at Nanmu's uninvited. He trusted their friendship to be deep enough for him to do that. He was anxious to see her and he boldly proclaimed it to her when he saw her. He told her to come and walk with him. Layla never knew Lee to be so forceful and she had mixed feelings about the way he approached her. Yet she didn't fight her feelings because she was happy to see him.

Nanmu's house was tucked away from other houses. The only entrance was a country dirt road about a quarter mile long and wide enough for only one vehicle. To get to that road one needed to travel a half mile down a gravel road that was right off the main highway. The traffic was usually light on the road except for the fisherman who frequents the pond that sits off the road. No one travels the dirt road except those who were visiting Nanmu.

They walked silently along the dirt road giving each other glances periodically. They didn't smile nor did they frown. They studied the other waiting to find the right words to break the silence.

"I don't like your hair. Why did you get rid of your curls?" Lee asked

She didn't respond; his comment annoyed her.

"Why have you been avoiding me?"

"I didn't want to hear you say, I told you so."

"Ma-Me, you know me better than that. You really think—"

"You were right Lee. It was nothing like what I expected. I should've listened to you."

"Did you meet your mother?" He asked softly.

"Oh, God, I don't want to talk about her," she crossed her arms and looked off into the woods.

They were silent again as they started walking along the gravel road. It was a pleasant day not sticky humid the way some Alabama days could be. While they walked along, comfortable in their silence, they noticed a gray pick up truck coming down the road toward them. It didn't concern them; they had walked pass the pond so they thought it was headed there. The truck started to speed up as it drew closer to them. The driver made a quick turn and stopped about a foot in front of them. Lee clutched Layla's hand and this provoked the driver. He jumped out of the truck; his partner that sat on the passenger side followed close behind him.

He was a red head tobacco chewing white man about six inches taller than Lee.

"What you doin wit that darkie gal?" He demanded.

I Blew God a Kiss

Lee whispered to Lalya and told her not to say anything.

"What you say boy?" He asked moving a little closer to Lee.

"You alright little lady?" The other fellow asked.

"I am fine," Layla said.

"This boy holding you against your will?" The tobacco chewer asked.

"No, he is my friend," Layla said moving a little closer to Lee.

"Why you got to be with this boy. White men not good enough for you?" He asked spitting tobacco at Lee's feet.

"I am black," Layla said boldly.

"Well shush my mouth. You hear that Baity," he said looking at the other guy, "A white coon! How many of ya'll is it back up in them woods?" He took a step forward and Lee pulled Layla aside.

"Baity you think she white all over," he reached out and tore Layla's top ripping her bra.

Lee stepped in front of Layla and cut the guy's arm with his switchblade.

"Come on!" Lee said swinging his blade.

The guy gripped his arm to stop the blood from gushing.

"Get in the truck Baity," he said to the other guy.

"You letting him get away with that. He can't take both of us."

"Don't count on it!" Lee yelled.

"In the truck now, Baity, you drive," he said backing up toward the truck.

Lee took off his shirt and wrapped it around Layla. She was

so shaken that Lee had to carry her.

When Lizzie saw them she ran frantically up to Lee accusing him of harming her niece. He tried to explain to her what happen but she would not listen. She went back in the house for Roy. He came out as Lee was carrying Layla up the stairs. In his boisterous manner Roy began swearing and threatening Lee. Layla screamed, "Please stop! Lee didn't hurt me." He sat her down and asked someone to get her something to drink.

"I just want to go lay down," she said sounding exalted.

Lizzie helped her to the bedroom. When she returned Nanmu was with her. Lee was explaining to Roy what happened.

"Do ya thank they be back?" Roy asked.

"No, I don't think so. I don't think they really wanted to hurt her. I think it just got out of hand."

"Lee do you feel you had to cut that man?" Nanmu asked sounding concerned.

"Nanmu what was he pose to do? He ripped that chile's shirt clean off," Lizzie said.

"I don't know Nanmu. I just reacted," Lee said.

"Better you than me. I liable to kilt one of 'em if it was me," Roy said.

"Don't talk like that. They are all God's children Roy," Nanmu said.

"Yes'em sorry," Roy was apologetic in respect to Nanmu, but deep down he was envious of Lee.

Layla locked herself in her room and would not open the door for anyone. Jordan was called to persuade her to come out.

"Ma-Me, it's Jay Pee, please open the door," Jordan said as

he knocked on the bedroom door. His family was standing behind him waiting to hear the response. He motioned them to go back. He heard Layla moving in the room, but she didn't open the door.

"Please Ma-Me, it's just me."

Layla opened the door. He noticed the blanket and pillow was on the floor. She returned to the spot she had on the floor and he joined her. She had used tissue paper balled up around her.

"I need you to be okay Ma-Me," Jordan said as he reached for her hand.

"I will never be okay."

"Why do you say that?"

"Lee tell you what happened."

"Yeah, that's just one person's opinion everybody don't think that way."

"Yes everybody do."

"That's not true. When anyone sees you they say, what a beautiful girl you are."

"That's only until they find out I have some black in me. I thought that if I changed my hair and became white that I would be happier. For a while I was. Nobody knew that I was from a black family," she opened her hand and showed him the card that she was clinging to.

"I was offered a chance to go to modeling school," she said.

"Ma-Me that is wonderful!"

"No it isn't, I don't want to go to school. I just want to die! I don't even know why I was born," she began to cry again.

"You listen to me. Remember what Nanmu always said that God created you for a purpose that only you can fulfill and that he don't make mistakes," Jordan said trying to console her.

"Well Nanmu is wrong. Me being black has done nothing but hurt me. All my life I have tried to fit in. I never did harm to nobody, but I keep getting hurt. God is punishing me. I know he is," she said still crying.

"Ma-Me God loves you. You are his special child."

"Why did he have to make people different colors? Why can't we all be the same color?"

"Come, go outside with me Ma-Me."

"I don't want to go," she said.

"Well stay there. I will be right back," he ran out of the house and started picking wild flowers and weeds, anything that had color to it. His family was asking if everything was okay. He assured them that all was well. He went back into the room to Layla with a hand full of flowers.

"Look Ma-Me, what do you see?"

"Jay Pee I don't want to play this game," her tone was dry.

"Really, what do you see?" He persisted.

"A bunch of weeds," she said less enthusiastic.

"Ma-Me, look at all the different colors. There are yellow ones and red and purple and white. So many, God is not a plain God—he gives us various colors in everything that he does so he is not going to make man all the same color."

She began looking through the flowers in his hand then she said, "I don't see any black ones."

He shook his head and said, "Ma-Me, don't you know that if you mix all the colors together you get black."

She started laughing and said, "Jay Pee, you can sell a polar bear a popsicle."

"Ma-Me, I want you to come back to New York with me."

"I don't know if I can do that."

"Listen it will be different this time. You won't be there alone. I have friends who are of mixed race like you. Some of them are from the south some where born in New York. They can help you and will be a great support for you."

"I need to tell you about what happened with Reggie."

"You don't have to talk about that."

"I want to. I feel like it was my fault. Not the kidnapping part but what he did to me," she hugged the pillow close to her. "He did not like black people. Someone hurt him when he was little and he took it out on the whole race. He was trying to force himself on me so I blurted out that I was black. He got enraged. It was like he was possessed or something. I was so scared. I knew I had messed up, but I didn't know how to take it back. Those men... today... with Lee," she paused, "how can I admit being black when it brings so much trouble?"

Jordan understood what she was saying and he knew there wasn't anything else he could say that would help her, but he knew of someone who could.

I Blew God a Kiss

Jordan asked Lee to sit with Layla until he returned. He needed to check on his mom and he had to convince Victoria to come to Alabama. When he stepped on the porch, Sam had arrived and was chatting with Roy. Nathan and Annie Mae were walking toward the house. Annie Mae joined Nanmu and Lizzie in the kitchen as they were preparing dinner.

Jordan sat with his uncles. He didn't talk, but he enjoyed the loudness of the one attempting to out talk the other. It seemed as if Roy was the dominant voice like a grizzly bear beating his chest for attention. Sam was normally quiet and observant. He was a school counselor, a good listener and the rational one. Nathan worked with his hands. He was masculine and intimidating. Roy, well Roy, he was just loud.

"Why you call me a lie," Roy honed in on his brother-in-law Sam.

"Man you like hearing yourself talk," Sam said.

"You don't speak good English and you talk more than anybody," Nathan said.

Nathan's remarks put fire in Roy and he began swearing and

waving his fist around like he wanted to hit him. Nathan apologized to him and told him he liked his stories. The comment calmed him.

"Ya mean it?" Roy asked with a smile.

"Yeah, man I mean it. That was a rotten thing to say," he gave Roy a high five.

"Well, did I ever tell ya' bout the time I went fishin' wit my ole Pappy?" Roy asked.

"You mean that time you caught that two feet catfish?" Sam asked.

"Nah, nah, not dat time. I lak fishin'. My brother Gary was wit us on the Tallapoosa. The warda was rough dat day and ah fishin' line kep gettin' caught up. I thought I had nabbed me a bass or somein. Pappy was yelling at me to ease up on the line. I'd ease and let loose," he was animated as he acted out the scene on the river with his hands; "Finely I saw it coming out the warda, it were a cooter. The biggest dang snapping tutter I ever saw. I were just bout to cut that line when I notice that thang had two head."

"Awe man, you had me until you said two heads," Nathan said.

"No man, I swar dat cooter had two head. My hook caught one of them heads and that other head was pulling trying to set him free."

"You are full of mess Roy," Sam said.

"Did I ever tell yall bout da day me and Lizzie got marred," Roy said.

Then they all became loud again all talking at once.

Jordan silently slipped away from his uncles. The fierce battle between them allowed him to go unnoticed. Their piercing voices resonated in his ears as he walked to his car. He smiled as he looked over his shoulder at them.

It took Victoria two days to arrive in Alabama. She had no desire to see Layla around the family, and she made sure that Jordan would be able to bring her to Mobile. She booked a suite at the Grand Hotel & Spa one of the most beautiful resorts in Alabama.

She made sure that she had a balcony room overlooking the lake draped by gorgeous greenery and flowers. She knew that Layla loved the outdoors so she picked the perfect spot for them to talk. Her hope was that Layla would be more receptive to her than she had been during their last meeting. She brought gifts for her and wanted to have the right time to present them to her. She did not want to seem as if she were buying her affection. She knew that Jordan was right about the reason she had given her daughter away, and it didn't have anything to do with money.

The extravagance of the hotel and the gardens surrounding it amazed Layla. She felt like Alice enclosed by a wonderful land of luxury. Jordan didn't stay with them, and Layla assured him that she would be fine.

"I have never seen anything as pretty as this," Layla said, as she leaned over the balcony looking at the lake.

Victoria stood beside her and asked if she wanted her to call room service to bring them something to eat. They ordered an array of seafood and cocktails to drink.

"Layla I have so much to say to you," Victoria said as they walked inside the suite.

"I feel that I owe you an apology for what I said to you when we first met," Layla said.

"Oh no, I deserved everything you said to me. I don't know what I was expecting from you. Jordan said you have been having a hard time trying to figure out your place in this world."

"That's an understatement."

"I don't want you to make the mistakes I made trying to please people. You need to be proud of who you are. Jordan said he asked you to come to New York with him. Would you like that?"

"I don't know," she brushed the hair out of her face.

"You have beautiful hair. Have you ever had a hair cut?"

"No, my mama…Sadie never wanted me to cut it. She said a woman's hair was her crown and glory."

"I know I brought her much pain, and I will always regret doing that to her. Layla you can't be angry with her. She did the best she could. She didn't have to take you as her own."

"What where you thinking giving me to my daddy knowing he had a family?"

"That's why I gave you to him because he had a family. I wanted you to have both parents. I was young and foolish. I let what people thought about me control the decisions I made. I guess I was afraid of disappointing my dad and my friends. I cared more about my reputation than my own daughter. You know Sadie called me once when you were nine—I think. She cursed at me saying some words I don't care to repeat. You were having trouble with a kid in school who was calling you names. She said you came home and put black shoe polish all over your body. She told me if she had anything to do with it. I would never be a part of your life. She loves you very much."

There was a knock at the door and Victoria let the room

service waiter in. She handed Layla her virgin Pina-colada and she ate the olive from her Margarita.

"I love lobster," she said looking at the spread in front of them, "do you?" Victoria asked Layla.

"Shrimp is my favorite," Layla said as she picked up a skewer.

"Ma-Me!" Victoria said as she began to sob.

Layla put the skewer down not understanding what just happened.

"Please forgive me," Victoria dried her tears with a napkin, "when I gave you to Joseph, I placed a gold bracelet on your arm with the inscription Ma-Me on it."

"Yeah, I still have that! Jay Pee gave it to me for my fifth birthday I put it on my favorite doll. I didn't know that was from you," Layla said surprised.

Victoria took a slow sip from her drink, "I wanted you to know that you would always be with me," she hugged her chest as she was speaking, "that's why I called you Ma-Me. Your name Layla Renee is from your great-grandmother who was a lovely dark haired French lady. She died when I was young. I have some pictures. Would you like to see?"

Layla nodded as tears flowed.

Victoria had four generations of pictures to show Layla. She wanted her to know all of her ancestry.

"Would you like to go to Paris to meet some of your cousins?" Victoria asked, not knowing what to expect from Layla.

"What do you want from me? I don't know you or these people. They're not my family. You are not my family."

"I am sorry. You're right, that was a lot to ask of you. You don't know me. Let me introduce myself. My name is Victoria Lynn Jospin Gentry," she extended her hand and Layla shook it, "I love my work. I am a defense attorney. I spend too much time at work and not enough time with my family. I have a gorgeous son name Michael who is the joy of my life. I enjoy classical musical and the Opera. I own a horse. Her name is Dancing Spirit. I ride her when I have a difficult case. Riding her helps me deliberate. I love lobster and Margaritas," she said getting up to fix her a fresh glass from the picture the waiter left for them.

"Is there anything you would like to know about me?" She asked.

"Did you ever regret your decision to give me up?"

"Everyday of my life," she paused, "Layla, I know I can't be your mother. You have a mother. I just want to get to know you, no strings, and no expectations. Can you accept that?"

"That's fair. I think I can do that," Layla said feeling a little more assured.

She spent the night with Victoria. She was awakened early the next morning by a phone call from Jordan. He asked if Victoria could have a driver bring her back to Grassy Creek as soon as possible. He said he would explain it all when she arrived. Layla feared that Nanmu's condition made a turn for the worst. She tried not to worry but her anxiety was getting the best of her. Jordan's tone over the phone was dramatic and urgent. It was a long drive to Grassy Creek and she desperately tried to calm herself. She concentrated on all that Victoria had shared with her. She felt a sense of wonderment about having another family and it overwhelmed her.

I Blew God a Kiss

She finally arrived at her parent's home. She was excited about seeing Sadie. She had so much she wanted to say to her. Her smile and excitement quickly dissipated when she gazed on Jordan's face. A cold chill rushed up her spine and pierced her soul as she hurried from the limo with her hand extended toward Jordan's.

"What's wrong?" She asked as she held onto his hand.

"We need to go to the hospital right away. Pop is there with Mama. She is in intensive care."

"She'll be alright Jay Pee, don't fret," she hugged and patted him on the back.

"Yes, Ma-Me, she will," Jordan cried.

As they walked down the hospital corridor it took an eternity to reach their destination. A young doctor was talking with Joseph as they walked up.

"Here is my son," Joseph said, "he has been with her. He'll be able to answer your questions."

"Hi I'm Dr. Bythe. I need to know if your mom has been portraying any of these symptoms," he held out a sheet and proceeded to ask him a list of questions.

"Has she shown any signs of mental confusions, irritability, drowsiness, poor temper control, headaches or muscle weakness?"

"Yes sir. She has all these. What does that mean?" Jordan asked.

"How long has she shown these signs?"

"I have been with her a little over a week and she has not been out of bed. I thought she was just depressed. My mom has never been sick."

"She's been sick," Joseph interjected, "she just didn't like her kids to know when she wasn't doing well. She's had these signs a long time. What do you think would cause these problems?"

"I believe she has Encephalitis—"

"What's that Encepfar…?" Jordan asked.

"Encephalitis, it is a swelling in the brain sometimes caused by an infection. I believe she's had it for a while. You need to contact the rest of your family. She's is in a coma and I don't believe she will wake up."

"No!" Layla screamed, "No, she will wake up! You are wrong! Please don't let her die!" She exclaimed to the doctor.

"There has to be something you can do for her. Can you call in a specialist?" Joseph asked.

"I am the specialist they called in. I am sorry. All I can do is to keep her comfortable."

Jordan pulled Layla close to him. They both were weeping.

"Jay Pee, I didn't tell her," Layla said.

"Tell her what Ma-Me?'

"I got to tell her Jay Pee. Where is she?" She asked the doctor.

The doctor walked them to her room. Sadie was inserted with a catheter in her veins and a tube ran through her nose. She had tubes running throughout her chest, one that prevented fluids from accumulating in her lungs. The fluids drained into a large plastic container near the foot of her bed.

Layla lay on her mother sobbing and pleading with her not to die. Jordan put his hand on Layla's shoulder and told her to talk to Sadie and let her know what she needed to tell her. Joseph handed her a wet cloth to dry her tears.

I Blew God a Kiss

"Mama, please hear me. I got something I want to tell you. I was wrong for running away. You are my mama and that's all that matters. I had a talk with Mrs. Vicky. I know you been mad at her. Please don't be mad no more she did the right thing giving me to you. She told me about when you called her. I remember that time when I put all that polish on me. You didn't get mad at me or nothing. You washed all that polish off me and said I was your special powder-puff child and I was never to try and change my complexion again. You always did that for me, made me proud of my color. Mama if you can hear me I just want to say thank you. Thank you for being my mama. I have not been a good daughter, but you been a good mama. Don't die mama. Give me a chance to do better."

I Blew God a Kiss

Layla stood on the red dirt mound that day reading the article written about her and reminiscing about all the times good and difficult she spent in Alabama. She wondered about her friend and hero Lee Sims who had moved away and whom she hadn't heard from in years. She thought about how she wanted to say thank you to him for being there for her.

The eloquently written article displayed all her accomplishments as a designer. It stated how Burdeau Manufactures would take on her designs. This would allow her clothing line to be distributed all over the world. She felt as if she was reading about someone else. She stood in the place where she had fantasized hundreds of times about making her name famous. And now Renée Designs had succeeded in doing that.

She remembered when Jordan asked her to come to New York with him. He was right, there were many people like her of mixed race; they were proud of their heritage and confident of whom they were as individuals. So many of them helped her to embrace the woman she had become. She held in her hand a scroll given to her by her best friend Sasha Cowen, her mother was German and her father black. It was an excerpt of Dr. Martin Luther King, Jr. "I Have a Dream," speech. She carried it with her even though she had it memorized. She especially held on to the statement that one day men would not be judged by the color of their skin but by the content of their character. Those words alone helped her to develop a character that was honorable.

Layla thought about all her struggles, many of them had kept her in bondage over the years. She was unable to forgive herself for running away during a time when her mother needed her most. She blamed herself for Sadie not recovering from her coma. Layla wished that she would have left with Jordan that night when he asked her to come home. She often wondered if Sadie heard her when she thanked her and asked her forgiveness. She had a new found respect for Joseph who moved back in the old house after Sadie died to take care of David, Juanita and her son Melvin Henry.

She looked down at her engagement ring and never imagined in a million years that she would be marrying her rescuer Frankie Petro. The wedding was to be held in Victoria's mansion with Nanmu Bailey and all the Bailey-Porter family in full support.

Years had passed since her talk with Sadie in that hospital; yet she was unable to let go of her regrets, until now standing on the familiar hill. For the first time in years, it was as if all the pain and loneliness she held on to had disappeared. She smiled as she gazed upon her favorite cloud and realized for the first time in her life that God had returned her kiss.

Acknowledgements

I would like to give honor to God and my Lord Jesus Christ, for giving me the strength and the courage to write this novel.

Being raised in a large, close-knit family was a sincere blessing. Being one of six girls, without brothers, I had many uncles who showered me with love and served as brothers and supplementary fathers. My love and passion for the Watts-Richard family provided me with a powerfully rich heritage that has given me a great appreciation for the simple things in life.

Special thanks to my family for giving me the inspiration to write.

Thank you Robert Mitchell, without your faith and encouragement I would have given up on this project.

Special thanks to my God given sister's for their valuable contribution; Lydia Smith, Rev. Delores Thompson, Dr. Shana James-Nzambele, Karen Porter, Adrienne Baughman, Lisa Young and Veronica Douglas.

Special thanks for the coaching skills of Deborah Lively and the editing skills of Danielle Watts and Barbara Henry.

Special thanks to my cover artist;
Model: Megan Richard
Photograph compliments of L. Davis of Simple Photography
Cover design and production layout by Detri Lively

How to Order
I Blew God a Kiss

Order additional copies of this novel as an ideal gift for family
and friends.

Please send me _____copies of your book at $14.95 each,
plus $3.00 shipping and handling per book ordered

Mail books to:
Name _____
Address_____
City_____State_____Zip_____

Send check or money order along with the above order
information to:
LHP Productions
P.O. Box 4062
Oak Park IL 60303
E-mail—lifehaspurpose@comcast.net
Website—www.LHPproductions.com
Please make checks and money orders payable to LHP Productions
Note: Order five or more books and receive free shipping!